Other books by William Sleator

Parasite Pig

PARASITE PIG

William Sleator

Dutton Children's Books
New York

Library of Congress Cataloging-in-Publication Data
Sleator, William.
Parasite Pig/William Sleator—1st ed.
p. cm.
Sequel to: Interstellar Pig.
Summary: Sixteen-year-old Barney, infected by an alien parasite,
and his friend Katie are taken to the planet J'koot by extraterrestrials intent
on playing the dangerous game known as Interstellar Pig.
ISBN 0-525-46918-4
[1.Games —Fiction. 2. Parasites—Fiction. 3. Science fiction.] I.Title.
PZ7.S6313 Par 2002
[Fic]—dc21   2002070881

Published in the United States by Dutton Children's Books,
a division of Penguin Putnam Books for Young Readers
345 Hudson Street, New York, New York 10014
www.penguinputnam.com

Designed by John Daly
Printed in USA
First Edition
1   3   5   7   9   10   8   6   4   2

For Judith Larner Lowry, a wonderful writer and friend,
who reminded me that biology exists

Acknowledgments

The author would like to thank Ida Kelsey, Rebecca Rodgers, Averil Way, and the students of International School Bangkok for their help with this book.

Parasite Pig

Prologue

In a hole there lived Madame Gondii. Not a dark, filthy, damp hole, with crawling things and an earthy smell, nor yet an arid, empty crumbly hole, with no place to sit and nothing to eat: it was the hole of Madame Toxoplasma Gondii, and that meant comfort.

She had a pretty door, though she never used it, since she was trapped inside her hole—until the major event of her life happened. She had a kitchen, where there was always something waiting for her to eat—and where she could excrete and mix her special hormones, too. Most important, she had a window, from which she could look out on the convoluted countryside. And there was light out there. She could see!

Madame Toxoplasma Gondii had it good. Other creatures had to explore in pitch darkness, using senses other than sight to gnaw and drill through muscle tissue and navigate their way through lightless branching rivers of blood to find their dark homes inside various organisms.

But the cyst in Barney's brain in which Madame Toxoplasma Gondii lived was ideally situated just beside his optic nerve, where the neural tissue was flooded with glorious light. She peered out to check on what Barney was looking at.

He was reading. And when she saw exactly *what* he was reading, her thing like a heart leapt with excitement. Back into her kitchen she scurried on her many legs, and began whipping up some very powerful hormones indeed.

Because convenient as this place was, it was not the home of her dreams, the real home she had to get to in order to survive—and have her babies.

1

Ten floors of stacks at Widener Library at Harvard were underground. To save money they kept them unlit; I pulled the ceiling lights on and off as I pushed my cart of books through the darkness.

The underground stacks were eerie, but I preferred them to the brighter upper floors. I felt protected here, less likely to get caught reading, instead of shelving the books nonstop, as I was supposed to do. Of course, Mrs. Donner, the boss, knew anyway if I didn't get back with the empty cart and pick up a new one within an hour. So it was a delicate balance. The longer I spent reading, the faster I had to shelve the rest of the books, or I'd get in trouble. She'd already threatened to fire me. And I didn't want to have to find an even *worse* job.

But I felt compelled to at least glance at the rule book

for the Interstellar Pig board game we were going to play this afternoon. It was only the board game, not the real game I'd played last summer on the beach. The alien game. It had been so horrifying—and exciting— that even now that it was over, I still wanted to play. The aliens last summer had been looking for an object called The Piggy. They would kill for it.

So it was really Zulma, Moyna, Jrlb, and the lichens' fault I had to have this job after school. Mom and Dad were making me work to help pay for the damage the aliens had caused to our rented beach house while they were trying to kill me. You can imagine Mom and Dad's reaction when I had tried to explain that the wrecked house wasn't *my* fault, that in fact I should be rewarded for saving the earth from those murderous creatures from outer space.

"You expect us to believe that? Shut up and get a job," was the nature of their response.

So here I was standing under a lightbulb in the dark underground stacks of Widener Library, snatching a few minutes to read about the planet J'koot in the Interstellar Pig rule book, a guide to all the species and planets involved in the game.

The natives of the planet J'koot are an unusually vicious species of intelligent crablike crustaceans. They are gourmets who especially relish dining on the delicately seasoned flesh of humanoid creatures. Because the planet has an Earth-like climate and a breathable atmosphere, two groups of humans from Earth secretly attempted to colonize it— Americans and Chinese. The Americans were meat-eaters, the Chinese ate a great deal of rice. Some of the crabs of J'koot preferred grain-fed meat, and so their prey was most often the Chinese. The Chinese male colonists observed the old custom of their people of wearing their hair in long queues, or braids. The crabs of J'koot liked their meat fresh. When they caught a Chinese man, they would hang him from a tree limb by his conveniently strong queue, and then break his legs and arms, leaving him alive and unable to move, hanging from the tree. Those crabs that preferred meat-fed Americans would simply break their legs and arms and leave them lying there helplessly on a rock. Their flesh, being in contact with the ground, got rotten faster than that of the hanging Chinese.

When the crabs were ready to feast, they would hack off one of the colonists' limbs and bear it away to season carefully and then eat, leaving the individual still alive, so the rest of the precious meat would continue to stay as fresh as possible. The rotten parts of the Americans' flesh had to be sliced off before amputation, of course without anesthetic, which would give the remaining edible meat a bad flavor. The agony endured by the colonists, both Chinese and American, was so extreme—

"Yes, nasty little planet, that," said a voice in the darkness close behind me. "Wouldn't want to end up *there*, would we now."

I jumped, and almost cried out. I hadn't heard anyone come up behind me to read over my shoulder. I spun around.

It was a stocky bald man much taller than me, grinning down engagingly. "Sorry, mate, didn't mean to give you such a start," he went on. "I just couldn't help being fascinated by good old J'koot."

"You've . . . heard of this place?" I asked him.

Why was I more curious than afraid, despite the way he had appeared out of nowhere in this dark place?

"Oh!" He put his hand over his mouth. "Well, er . . ." he mumbled, sounding a little confused, "I have to confess, I'm a science fiction fan. In fact, that's why I'm poking around in here. Do you happen to know a bloke named Barney?"

"*I'm* Barney," I said, without hesitation.

"The same Barney who posted the notice about the game?"

Now I understood. "Oh, you're interested in playing?" I asked him.

"Very much indeed," he said, beaming more broadly down at me.

"That's great. We could use another player. In fact, we're having a session today, when I finish working."

"Count me in, mate," he said. "Julian's the name."

"Hi," I said, and extended my hand.

But he kept his hands behind his back. That was odd; his smile wasn't the least bit rude. But he did have some kind of an accent. Maybe he was from a country where people didn't shake hands. Anyway, I was glad he had come along, whether he shook my hand or not. The game would be more exciting with a fourth player.

The aliens had brought the board game with them when they moved into the cottage next to ours. We had played several rounds at their cottage, and I was flattered that they had included me. In their human disguises they were three very glamorous and attractive people. My parents were as taken in by them as I was, at first.

But the last time we played, they had plotted to keep my parents stuck away from home in a storm, and then had brought the board and the cards and the pieces over to our house. They wanted to play there, because they knew I had found the *real* Piggy, the prize of their real game, and that it was hidden in our house. We had started by picking character and attribute cards from the game set, as usual. Then they had assumed their true alien forms, and the game suddenly became real. They did everything they could to kill me—one had a razor-sharp sword growing out of its head; others had venom and sticky cables and suckers, not to mention nasty weapons.

The aliens all believed that the player who had The Piggy at the end of the game would be the only survivor, and that everyone else would die. But I knew better. I had figured out that The Piggy was duping all of them, that it had created this pointless game because it wanted to be wanted by all the species.

The Piggy was a spherical pink object with one eye and a smiling mouth. Its smile somehow managed to be vapid and menacing at the same time. It always gave me a jolt when I saw its face on the board-game card.

In the end, the sapient carnivorous lichen from the planet Mbridlengile (I was the only one who was immune to them) had ended up with The Piggy, and beamed themselves and it up to their ship before the others could stop them. And so Zulma, Moyna, and Jrlb had taken off so fast after the lichen that they had left the board game and all the cards and pieces at our beach house. I kept it, and brought it home when we moved out of the cottage.

I left it in the bottom of my closet for a while, not looking at it. I had mixed emotions about it. Playing the game had been exciting at first. Then it had become terrifying. But in the end the memory of the excitement—and how I had saved myself and the world—won out. I had gotten the board game out and looked at it only a few weeks ago. And I decided that I couldn't get killed or destroy the earth by playing the board game with other humans. After all, the board game had not been deadly at all until the *aliens* had decided to start playing for real.

So I put up a notice on the Widener Library bulletin board and a community Web site, briefly describing the game and asking if anyone wanted to play, and giving my e-mail address. So far, two others had started playing with me, another sixteen-year-old high-school student who worked shelving books, named Katie, and a Harvard undergraduate named Matt. They had both really gotten into the game in the few weeks we'd been playing, and we were all looking for a fourth player to make it even more fun.

And now we had finally found one. Julian seemed older, and he had to be a graduate student or teaching assistant in order to get into the stacks, but that was fine—as long as he turned out to be a good player.

I did wonder why he hadn't e-mailed me, since that was the way the notices said to reach me. And it was odd how he had just happened to stumble across me in the stacks. But something made me dismiss these concerns. What mattered was a good fourth player—and the fact that Julian was a science fiction fan was a positive indicator.

I looked at my watch. "Yikes! I've got to get back to work or I'll be in big trouble," I said. "We play in an undergraduate's apartment—we can't play in the library because it would disturb the people studying. We're meeting at 23 Green Street, apartment 2A, at four-thirty," I told him, not even thinking to worry that Matt might not want me to give his address to a total stranger before checking with him. "Matt Rosen is the name of the guy who lives there."

"Lovely. See you then, mate," Julian said.

I was about to ask him what his affiliation with the university was. But he faded into the darkness as suddenly and silently as he had arrived.

2

"I just think it's peculiar that he found you so easily, in all ten floors of those underground stacks," Katie said as we walked down the broad steps of Widener Library in the November late afternoon darkness.

Katie was another book-shelver, sixteen years old, like me. Meeting her was the best thing about having this job. We weren't exactly going out, but we usually had coffee or something together after work, and had gotten to be pretty good friends. She was an excellent player of Interstellar Pig.

I knew that Katie's family was not as well-off as mine, and they lived in a fringe neighborhood in the city, not out in the peaceful suburbs where we lived. She was tougher and more straightforward than most girls I knew. I liked that. And she was more practical than I was.

She was also very cute.

I shrugged. "So it was a coincidence that he ran into me. That happens. What matters is that we have a fourth player now. I'm telling you, the game is way better with four than three."

We had reached busy Massachusetts Avenue. Katie pushed back her short wavy dark hair then pulled her jacket more tightly around her as we waited for the traffic light to change.

She shook her head. "We'll see. If he doesn't work out, we'll have to drop him. There's something I don't like about it."

Of course I hadn't told Katie or Matt that the board game we were playing had become vicious reality last summer. They'd think I was crazy. So it was interesting that Katie was so suspicious of this new guy, Julian. But I was pretty sure she'd get to like him. He had been very pleasant and polite, and was obviously into science fiction. If he was a good player, she and Matt would have to accept him.

We crossed the street.

Matt was a senior, and seniors could have their own apartments instead of living in the Harvard houses. He lived in a three-story wooden building in need of repair, several blocks from the campus. Matt's apartment had a living room, two bedrooms, and a small kitchen and bathroom. The couch and chairs in the living room were threadbare and sagging, obviously from a thrift shop. There was very little else in the apartment, except for some textbooks, but we figured that was the way college students lived.

What was important was that there was a big table,

perfect for playing the game, and Matt's roommate was in so many clubs and teams that we had never even seen him. We were very lucky to have found Matt.

Julian hadn't arrived when we got to Matt's place. "We have a fourth player," I told Matt as soon as he opened the door. But I was worried. What if Julian didn't show up? That would be really disappointing.

"A person who answered the ad?" Matt said, adjusting his glasses. They were big with very thick, black rims that made his eyes seem unusually large.

"Well, he saw the ad, and then . . . he just happened to find me in the stacks while I was working this afternoon," I said.

Matt and Katie exchanged a look.

"Yeah. Funny coincidence," she said. "Something about it I don't—"

There was a gentle knock on the door.

Matt hesitated for longer than I liked, and I almost pulled the door open myself, but managed to wait until Matt did. Julian, stocky and bald and a head taller than any of us, stood there grinning in a lopsided way, the right side of his mouth higher than the left. In his huge oversized parka he looked even bulkier than he had in the stacks. He also seemed slightly fuzzy around the edges. Was there something wrong with my eyes?

"Well, I see I've found the right place. Very nice to meet you all," Julian said pleasantly.

"This is Katie, and this is Matt," I said. "And this is Julian."

They all said hello. I was embarrassed by how slowly and ungraciously Matt beckoned to him to come in.

Matt had already set up the board, the pieces, the three sets of cards, and the timer on the table. I gestured at it as I got the fat rule book out of my backpack. "There's Interstellar Pig," I said to Julian.

For a big guy, Julian moved very quickly. The three of us watched him as he bent over the game, avidly taking it all in. The board *was* pretty spectacular, with the planets somehow appearing to be floating above it, and the pathways of stars glowing unblinking as they would in outer space.

And then I noticed: There was a planet on the board that had not figured in the game we played last summer, a planet as blue and green and inviting as Earth.

"J'koot," Julian said. "Barney and I were reading about it just this afternoon. Beautiful planet, that. Dangerous, too."

"Beautiful?" I said, staring down at it in fascination. "It didn't say that in the rule book." But somehow I already knew he was right. I decided to head for J'koot as soon as we started playing—I didn't care how dangerous it was. I had to get there.

"How do *you* know about it?" Katie demanded of Julian.

"I told Barney. I'm a longtime follower of science fiction." Julian rubbed his hands together. "Can we start playing now, please?"

"But . . . what were you doing in the Widener stacks?" Katie wanted to know. "You have to have a special pass to get in. Are you a graduate student or an instructor or what?"

"Oh," Julian said, his eyes not meeting hers. "Oh, yes, that. Righty-oh. I'm . . . doing a special research project. I got permission from the university. Can we play, please?"

Matt and Katie exchanged another glance. Obviously they didn't believe Julian. But so what? I was as eager to play as he was.

"Come on, let's deal the character cards," I said, sitting down and putting the rule book on the table. Julian shrugged off his parka, pulled up a chair, and sat beside me.

The other two sat down slowly across from us, both looking uneasy. What was their problem? Anyway, it was my game, so who got to play it was up to me. I had the feeling that if they hadn't known that, they might have tried to get Julian out of here.

I shuffled the character cards and dealt one to each player, facedown. When I turned over my card, there it was again—the realistic drawing of me, and the words *Homo sapiens*. No matter who shuffled or dealt the cards, every time we played I drew this one. Matt and Katie were still bothered by this statistically impossible coincidence, but there was nothing for them to do but accept it, if they wanted to keep playing.

Matt and Katie drew different cards every time we played. This time Matt got Jrlb, a water-breathing gill man from Thrilb, and Katie got Zulma, the brilliant and hideous spider lady from Vavoosh. They were two of the aliens I had played with last summer, and I was almost expecting Julian to draw Moyna, the octopuslike gas bag from Flaeioub, who was another alien I had dealt with.

Instead, he drew a card none of us had ever seen before. The picture showed a long, twisted worm with a head covered by sharp curving spikes. The name of the species was *Guanophilia lutansia.*

"A new species," Katie muttered, and reached for the rule book. She looked up the species, and obviously it had appeared there, too, because she read for a moment, then glared directly at Julian. "It's a parasitic tapeworm. It can inhabit the intestines of many different creatures from many different planets, preferring reptile, canine, and sometimes humanoid species." She paused. "Its IRSC is 53. And its personal name is Julian."

"Well, this game is just *full* of jolly little surprises, isn't it," Julian said brightly, obviously trying to make light of this new, startling coincidence.

Matt and Katie looked numbly at each other. I didn't care. "Okay, so it's a coincidence," I said. "Now can we *please play?*"

Katie dealt out the attribute cards, which were weapons and breathing gear and poisons and antidotes and bombs and other equipment, and one of them was The Piggy. In the real live game you could pick your own equipment, but in the board game you had to make do with what was dealt to you.

Let's say you were me, *Homo sapiens,* an oxygen breather. That meant that unless you were dealt a breathing device, you could not land on any planets that did not have an atmosphere rich in oxygen—and that would limit you a lot. Each species had its own limitations. Matt, for instance, was Jrlb, the fish man, who could only breathe water. If he didn't have cumbersome water-breathing equipment, he was stuck in the oceans, wherever he went. Unless, of course, he had the hyperspace card, which would allow him to engage in combat on land, jumping back to the ocean through hyperspace whenever he needed another gulp of water to breathe.

Your attributes were kept secret from the other players.

I saw immediately that I did not get The Piggy. That meant I had to watch the other players carefully and try to figure out which one of them *did* have it.

I did not get any oxygen-breathing equipment either, but that was okay because when I double-checked the rule book, I saw that the atmosphere and climate of J'koot were almost exactly the same as Earth's. And J'koot was the only planet I was interested in going to. It was not really a matter of strategy to go there; I just wanted to, for some reason I could not explain.

What I *did* have was the Portable Access to the Fifth-Dimensional Matrix. Just as the hyperspace card took you out of normal space so you could go anywhere in an instant, the Fifth-Dimensional Matrix took you out of time so you could go any*when* you wanted to be. This could be very useful in certain situations. I also had a heat pump, which I would not need on J'koot, a grenade, and a virulent bacteria called *Lanthrococcus molluscans,* which was fatal to many of the species in the game, including myself. I did not, however, have the vaccine, which would protect *me* from it. That meant I had to hide the bacteria on some planet I wasn't going to myself, but that I expected one or more of the other players to land on—and then get sick and die.

I had a laser gun—there were lots of those. If two players with similar guns were in direct combat, the outcome was determined by their intelligence—the smarter one won. The intelligence of all the species was quantified by the Interstellar Relative Sapience Code—referred to as the IRSC—and the weird thing about it was that the *lower* the number, the higher the intelligence. Mine was 93.7. That put me at a big disadvantage, since Zulma's was 10, Jrlb's was 16, and Julian's was 53, meaning each one of them would beat me if we were in direct combat with a similar weapon.

I had other stuff in my hand that I wouldn't need on J'koot. I also had a rope and a flashlight, always useful, and very luckily I had some freeze-dried food that *Homo sapiens* could eat. I also had the instant jungle seed, which when thrown behind me would immediately become a junglelike barrier that would slow down any pursuers—except the lichen, who could eat through anything.

Matt laid out the planet envelopes. We rolled the dice to determine who would choose first. Julian won. I was second. The first planet he picked, without hesitation, was J'koot.

I cursed him inwardly. You could only carry six attribute cards in your hand, but you could store the others in planet envelopes and use them when you got to those planets on the board.

I tried to figure out his strategy as he quickly chose a couple more planet envelopes. Zulma and Jrlb could not go to J'koot without breathing gear. Only I would be comfortable there. What did that mean about Julian's choice?

Since I couldn't get J'koot and didn't have The Piggy to hide, I was not too picky about the planets I chose. I distributed my attributes according to which oncs I would need if I was forced to land on any of these particular planets. Matt and Katie packed their envelopes.

Katie put her piece, a little black spider, on Vavoosh, her home planet. Matt put his on Thrilb and I put mine on Earth. Julian put his, a pinkish wormlike thing, on Voeves.

Katie grabbed the rule book and looked up Julian the tapeworm again. "How did you know you originated on Voeves?" she demanded. "I didn't read that part out loud."

He shrugged and giggled uncomfortably. "Made a lucky guess, I suppose."

Katie and Matt were glowering at him again. But now at last we could play. I held my hand above the round white timer. You could not choose how long a period of time you wanted to play. The timer couldn't be controlled and was completely random—sometimes it went off in ten minutes, sometimes in thirty. When it did go off, the species who had The Piggy in its hand won, and lived. All the other species died, and their planets were destroyed—until the next game. It was very intense because you could see how fast the timer was going; the faster it went, the faster you had to move in order to get The Piggy before it went off.

"Everybody ready?" I asked, my hand poised to start it.

They all nodded, with the expressions of runners on the starting block just before the gun.

I pressed the timer and the game was on.

The order of play was determined by more rolls of the dice. This time I won, and moved first. I rolled a 9, and moved nine stars along the complex pathway toward

J'koot. Zulma and Jrlb moved next. It was hard to tell so early what planets they were headed for. Julian rolled last and moved six stars from Voeves in what seemed to me the direction of J'koot.

The star he landed on began to blink as soon as he put his piece down upon it. He didn't seemed startled by this.

"That means you have to take an instruction card," I said. "You pick them out of that slot in the center of—"

He was already pulling the card out. It seemed more and more obvious that Julian must have played this game before—this alien game that I had thought was the only one on Earth.

But how did I know this was the only one on Earth? Other aliens could have been here, too, and brought their own sets. It was just another coincidence. I couldn't ruin my game by letting myself worry about it.

Julian read the card and then chuckled. "Well, well, my lucky day," he said, and read the instruction card aloud: "You just hit an invisible wormhole through hyperspace. Go directly to the planet you wish to travel to."

I cursed silently again as he gleefully plopped his piece down on J'koot, and immediately began exchanging cards between those in his hand and those in the J'koot envelope.

I checked the timer. The black semicircle had already engulfed almost a fourth of the white surface. It was going really fast today.

And then I rolled a lousy 3. I began to feel frantic—I was going nowhere and there wasn't much time. I moved three little stars in the direction of J'koot.

And landed on a blinking star.

21

I dreaded what the instruction card would say. Julian had been lucky. These cards were more likely to tell you something like, "Failure in communications system. Go directly into orbit around the nearest planet and spend the next three turns making repairs."

I picked the card and read it. And then I laughed louder than Julian had. "Interstellar winds have blown you into the nearest hyperspace wormhole. Go directly to the planet of your choice."

Now Julian was the one to be suspicious. For the first time he looked at me with an unfriendly expression, his mouth hard, his jaw jutting out. "There aren't very many—I mean, there *shouldn't* be very many instruction cards so similar, and especially not right next to each other like that. Who shuffled those cards anyway?"

"*I* shuffled them," Katie told him, "and they were shuffled fairly. I don't cheat." We all glanced nervously at the timer, which was now three-eighths of the way across. "Play!" Katie ordered.

My heart lifted as I landed on the rolling green hills of J'koot. The game was so intense that it always seemed you were really *on* a particular planet. I felt positively euphoric being here.

But I couldn't relax. There were those crabs that ate human flesh. And Julian was here, too, which most likely meant direct combat—and if he had The Piggy, we'd be fighting for sure.

But how did you fight with a tapeworm?

Then I saw something in the distance. Not a crab and not a tapeworm. Something that looked a whole lot like a dinosaur. I remembered from what Katie had read in the rule book that the intestines of reptiles were first on the list of where this tapeworm preferred to reside. I watched the dinosaur as it approached. Was Julian living in its intestine?

It seemed to be moving very quickly through the tall grasses, especially for something so big. Julian was big and he moved quickly, too—that's where I must have gotten the idea the dinosaur would be fast. As it got closer, I could see that it was not exactly like any of the earth dinosaurs I was familiar with. What it was most similar to was a velociraptor, those vicious creatures with claws and big teeth that could run faster than any human. Only this thing was more dangerous because its front claws were more highly developed, with five digits, like human hands.

I gulped, the euphoria quickly draining away.

Whether Julian had The Piggy or not, I had to kill the dinosaur, just in order to stay alive. And if Julian *did* have The Piggy, then as soon as his host creature was dead, I'd be able to get it from either the cards in Julian's hand or the envelope for this planet. Then I'd win—Zulma and Jrlb were way too far away to get here in time to fight me.

All I had to do was kill the dinosaur, which, in my imagination, was looking bigger and bigger the closer it got. And now I could see that it had a laser gun in one claw and a neural whip in the other.

I remembered that Julian's IRSC was way better than mine. That meant I'd lose for sure if I tried to fight the creature with my laser gun. I had stashed the bacteria on another planet, and anyway, the bacteria would kill me as well as him.

That left me with the grenade. It could have been

worse. The grenade was powerful and would kill the dinosaur easily. The difficulty was to know exactly when to pull out the pin and to aim and throw it accurately.

And I had sure never been picked to pitch on a baseball team.

The next second I knew I had to throw the grenade soon. In moments, the dinosaur would be so close that the grenade would kill me, too. I pulled the pin out with my teeth and spit it out. I raised my arm to throw. The grenade would go off in ten seconds. I forced myself to do nothing and count slowly to five as the dinosaur got closer and closer. I took careful aim, my eyes on the dinosaur's, and threw.

And threw well. The grenade was heading right for the dinosaur's neck. I started to turn and run from the blast.

But before I could, the dinosaur raised one of its small arms and with the back of its claw batted the grenade with great force back in my direction.

Too much force. The grenade sailed right over my head and went off far enough behind me that, in my imagination, I only felt the ground shake and a few pebbles hit my neck.

In the next second, from a hole in the ground I had not seen, came the lichen—the sapient carnivorous lichen from the planet Mbridlengile. They were the most loathsome and dangerous species in the game, a bubbling pink smear made up of uncounted individual cells that could eat anything alive. There was no way to communicate with them unless you were immune to them. In the real game, I *had been* immune to them, which was largely what kept me alive. But in this board game I wasn't.

How had they gotten here? No one had picked them as a species. Could you store a *species* on a planet? I hadn't known that. But someone else had. And now the lichen were eating me, slowly and painfully. My toes were gradually dissolving away in burning acid. Things had moved fast and there was probably enough time in the game for them to put me through a lot of agony before I died.

But I still had the Portable Access to the Fifth-Dimensional Matrix. Even while screaming in pain as the lichen ate me, I somehow managed to pull it out, set it, and press ACTIVATE. It took me instantly to the end of the game, and the timer went off, terminating my pain.

Julian and I stared at each other as the timer rang. His expression had changed again. He was looking at me differently than before, speculatively, his lips partly open, his tongue visible. It was a hungry look.

The spell broke when the timer stopped. Julian sat up straighter and beamed around at everyone, rubbing his hands again. "Jolly good, jolly good!" he exclaimed. "What fine players you all are!"

We looked instantly at the board. Earth, Vavoosh, and Thrilb were gone. Voeves remained. Julian took a card from his hand and displayed it. The round pink face, the single eye in the middle, the vapidly smiling mouth. The Piggy.

"But how did the lichen get on J'koot?" I wanted to know. "They're not even playing this game—nobody picked them. I didn't know you could hide a *species* on a planet."

Julian looked very smug. "Well, now you know. An advanced trick. Do let's play again, right away!" he said eagerly.

"No time," Katie said. "Barney and I have to get home, and before that we need to have a meeting." She stood up.

"And my roommate will be returning soon," Matt added sourly. I had never heard him use that tone of voice before.

"Oh, I get the picture," Julian said, standing up. "When do we next play again?"

"We have this rule about accepting new players," Katie said, making up the rule on the spot. "We have to play one game, and after that the original players discuss the new player—in private."

I thought she was being a little harsh, but I also didn't want to argue with her in the mood she was in now.

And Julian got the idea that Katie and Matt, at any rate, wanted him to leave right away. He turned to me. "Put in a good word for me, Barney. That was an exciting match the two of us had, and I'd like another. Can I e-mail you to find out?"

"Sure . . . er, sure," I said.

"Righty-oh," he said, slipping into his parka. He lifted one hand. "Hope to see you all again. Byeeeeeee." And he was out the door.

I turned back to Katie and Matt. "Well?" I said.

"No way," Katie said. Matt shook his head vehemently, agreeing with her.

I was baffled—and angry. "But he was such a good

player! He beat us all on his first game. You can't argue with that. Come on!"

"That's the whole problem," Katie said, and Matt nodded. "He's played it before—and he didn't tell us. *Why* didn't he tell us? What's he hiding from us? Why does he have to lie? I don't like liars."

Katie didn't even know the real significance of what she was saying: that if he had played it before, he could very easily be one of the gaming species, another alien who was already part of the game, and who was drawing me back into the *real* game again—the deadly one. Maybe she *was* right. Did I really want to get involved with Zulma and Moyna and Jrlb, and the lichen again, and now Julian and his dinosaur?

How much did Julian guess—or know—about me, anyway?

And why was I so reluctant to drop him, even now that I knew he could put me into real danger?

"I . . . I guess you're right," was all I could think of to say.

"I wish he didn't know your e-mail address," Katie said. She sounded really worried. "You didn't tell him your phone number or address or anything, did you?"

"No."

"That's good. But Barney. He lied. And I think he wants something. From you. Did you get that feeling, too, Matt?"

"He lied for sure," Matt said angrily. "And he's too much intrigued. There's something behind it. Something he wants that he's not mouthing." He pushed his large glasses back abruptly.

Now they were getting me even more scared, even

27

though they didn't know how dangerous a *real* game-player could be.

Katie and I left Matt's together. And when we parted at the subway station, she said, "See you tomorrow—and keep all your doors and windows locked."

"I will," I said, and meant it.

Madame Gondii could see better than Barney in the darkness and had sensed Julian looking for him in the library. She had helped Julian find Barney by excreting special scent hormones, and she was still pouring them into Barney now so that Julian could smell Barney easily. She knew Julian had ways of not being noticed when he didn't want to be. The scent hormones she was sending out helped him to keep track of Barney and to be even more discreet in this task.

The cyst in Barney's brain in which Madame Toxoplasma Gondii lived was what hid and protected her from his immune system.

She was a sprightly segmented little thing with a large number of underdeveloped tentacles and several mouths. Right now she didn't need the tentacles—they would grow out later. She used one of her mouths to drink Barney's blood, which kept her alive, and another mouth to excrete her special hormones and make them into recipes. She had several multifaceted eyes.

For the last month or so she had stopped watching when Barney was going home on the subway—it was boring, the same thing every day. But this evening she watched. For a change Barney was not reading. He was looking around at the other people on the subway car. She wasn't happy about that. She would have liked to give him some hormones to impel him to take the book from his pocket, but she had to keep sending out the scent hormones, and that required all her concentration. She very much hoped Julian would not lose track of Barney.

Hoping made her irritable. Hoping was not her thing. She preferred complete control. And some of the time, even here, she had it. But dealing with both creatures at once taxed her powers and made her nervous. She did what she could to stifle her irritability—moods didn't help with the hormone measuring and mixing and excretion processes.

And she was frustrated as well as nervous. She wanted so much to be totally in charge. But here, in this particular temporary home, in this particular organism, she couldn't be.

Only if she reached her eventual goal and her *real* home would she be entirely in control at all times. Only there would she be able to have her babies, the most important function of her life. That was why she had to subdue her emotions now, and keep sending out the scent hormones to Julian.

Because in a certain way, she and Julian were both after the same thing.

4

I plodded up the dark hill from the Green Line station to our house, feeling more frightened than I'd ever been on this daily walk. The more I thought about it, the more sure I was that Julian had to be an alien game-player in disguise. And somehow, he had found me.

Yes, the Interstellar Pig adventure had been exciting, but when the aliens had finally left, what I felt more than anything else was profound relief that I'd lived through it—they were violent and demented and had almost killed me *several* times.

So why did I want to put myself at risk again?

And why did I keep thinking about J'koot, and how lovely it was there?

I kept looking back at the shadows of the trees swaying behind me. No one seemed to be following me, but it wasn't easy to tell for sure—the lights were far apart on this street. I was relieved when I reached our front door, which we didn't usually lock until Mom and Dad went to bed. This evening I locked it.

Our little shih tzu, Chang, was waiting for me, looking up and eagerly wagging his tail. He was a well-behaved creature, hardly bigger than a cat, who didn't bark and didn't shed—otherwise Mom would never have allowed him in the house.

Interior decorating was one of Mom's hobbies and she was very proud of the way she had done our home. I spent time at many of my friends' houses and I could see now that Mom's taste was fussy—frilly curtains, too many knickknacks on little tables, and the slipcovers and rugs and wall colors matched too perfectly. The entrance hallway was all greens, the living room all peach and creamy, and everything always had to be perfectly in place. I actually felt more comfortable in other people's houses.

Mom and Dad had been angry about the damage done to the rental house, so angry that I couldn't worm my way out of getting the after-school job. If anything like that happened to our real home, it was hard to imagine how deep an emotional trauma it would be for Mom.

On the other hand, she would then have an excuse to do it up all over again, and I almost chuckled, feeling frivolous for a moment at getting safely home.

I put down my books on the green table in the front hall and shrugged out of my jacket.

Mom came out of the kitchen in her pink-and-white ruffled apron, a wooden spoon in her hand. She leaned against the door with her hand on her hip. "Were you out with your little friend what's-her-name again?" she asked me. "I know you get out of work at five."

I tried not to sound irritated by her questions—I *was* sixteen. "You know Katie and I go to Peet's Coffee after work," I said. I actually got out of work at four, but wisely had told Mom it was five from the beginning.

"I wish you'd bring her here sometime," Mom said. "I like to know what kind of kids you're hanging out with."

"Mom, I'm sixteen, I'm responsible. You'd like Katie a lot."

"I'm not so sure anymore, after whatever it was that got into you last summer." She stood up straight. "And don't leave your books lying around like that."

I sighed. I saved the Earth from those aliens and she treats me like a baby? "I haven't had a chance to bring them up to my room. I just got home." I picked up the books and started upstairs.

"And don't dawdle," she added. "I made *soufflé aux fruits de mer* and I'm just about to take it out of the oven."

I cringed at her terrible French accent.

Dad and I sat at the shining wooden table in the lavender dining room as Mom brought in the soufflé. It had puffed and risen a good two inches above the dish.

"It looks wonderful, dear," Dad said.

Mom glanced at me after she carefully set it down at her place. "Yeah, looks great," I said dutifully.

She served it delicately, pulling it apart with two spoons so it would deflate as little as possible. The salads

33

were carefully arranged in separate bowls, one for each of us, and the hot French bread was wrapped in a lavender napkin in a wicker basket. Mom and Dad each had a small glass of wine—none for me, of course.

I remembered the summer meal with Zena, Manny, and Joe, who had later become Zulma, Moyna, and Jrlb—lobster, fresh green beans and new potatoes, lime pie and champagne. It had been eaten on chipped plates in a crummy pink cement-block cottage, but it was so much more relaxed and fun than this meal. Not to mention more delicious. Mom had a habit of putting sugar in everything, certainly in the salad dressing and maybe even some in the soufflé. She tried to be a gourmet cook, but she didn't have the flair for it that Manny had.

Then I remembered the vile creature Manny had turned into.

"The soufflé is delicious, dear," Dad said.

"Mmm," I agreed, though it was, in fact, a little sweet. And I wasn't too happy about the crabmeat in it, thinking of the nasty gourmet crabs on J'koot.

"Well, how was school and work today, Barney?" Dad said.

"Fine."

"You didn't get in trouble again for reading, I hope."

I cursed myself for ever telling them about that. "No," I lied. "And Friday is payday, so I'll have another check for you then," I added, hoping to get off the subject and onto something they might like.

"Well, I think you're learning an important lesson. You may grow up to be like those fine neighbors we had last summer."

"Yeah," was all I could say. I had tried and tried to convince them that the neighbors were aliens, but they had been so dazzled by them, and anyway they just weren't capable of stretching their minds to that extent. They believed I'd had some kind of mental breakdown and trashed the house for no reason, or maybe because Mom and Dad had left me alone during the storm. At least the people at the clinic they sent me to had told them I was fine after only three days—I hadn't made the mistake of trying to tell *them* about the aliens. I said the storm had damaged the house, and they could see right away how fussy and uptight Mom was.

I heard what sounded like a footstep upstairs. "What was that noise?" I said quickly.

They looked at each other. "It's November, Barney," Mom said. "There's some wind. That makes things creak."

I hoped she was right.

I went upstairs after supper while Mom cleaned up and Dad watched TV. Before tackling the math set that was due tomorrow, I decided to play a few rounds of a game I'd started the night before. I clicked the mouse on my computer, but when the screensaver dissolved, the game didn't appear. Instead there were some astonishingly gross pictures of worms with several different kinds of twisted, spiky heads, some with long gooey suckers on them, some very convoluted, some with sharp, dangerous-looking hooks like Julian's character in the game. The caption said that there were more than five thousand species of tapeworms that live in the intestines of various animals, including humans, some of them sixty feet long, and that their heads were all different in order to help them cling to the bodies of their specific hosts. They usually got inside them through contaminated food.

Who but Julian would have put these threatening pictures on my computer? That had to mean he had gotten into the house—and that I wasn't safe, even here. I got rid of the page immediately.

But now I felt uncomfortable even in my own room. I called Katie.

"Barney, Matt followed me home," she said, before I even had a chance to tell her what had happened to me.

"*Matt?* Are you sure?"

"Yeah, I'm sure," she said, sounding irritated that I would even question her. And I believed her; I knew she was a lot more streetwise than I was. "Why would he do that?" she continued. "If he wanted to know where I live, why didn't he just ask? He got off the subway at my stop and kept behind me. Every time I looked around he was there, but trying to hide, looking the other way, pretending he didn't see me. I started to go back to ask him what he was doing and he turned around and walked toward the subway like I wasn't there. It was so *weird.* I didn't know what to do. He was acting so funny I didn't want to just *lead* him to our apartment, but what choice did I have? I wanted to get home ASAP. So now he knows where I live. And he doesn't want me to know he knows."

It *was* strange. Matt had never done anything peculiar like that before. What had gotten into him today?

"Well, Julian knows where I live," I said. "And he's been in here. I kept thinking somebody might be fol-

36

lowing me when I got off the train, too. And then I heard this noise upstairs while we were eating, but of course Mom and Dad said it was nothing. But then my computer wasn't on the right program. It was like on an encyclopedia page about these disgusting tapeworms, with horrible pictures."

"You're *sure* you didn't leave the computer there yourself?"

"Sure I'm sure. Somebody brought up those pictures on my computer. And who else could it be?"

"Maybe he wasn't really inside your house. Maybe he just e-mailed those pictures to you."

I sighed. "E-mail doesn't work that way, and you know it. I wasn't logged on."

There was silence for a little while. "I guess . . . everybody would think you were being hysterical if you called the police," she finally said.

"They already think that anyway, because of something that happened last summer." For some reason I *still* didn't want to tell her. "They'd just say I'd done it myself, or else it was a computer malfunction."

"Maybe that's all it was," she said hopefully. "Computers get screwed up all the time. Mine is definitely fickle and hates humans."

"Maybe," I said doubtfully. "Except it's never done anything like this before. And why tapeworms?"

"He's a sicko. Check the whole house and then make sure all your doors are locked," she said.

"Thanks," I said. "That makes me feel a lot better."

"What can I say? You never should have invited him. I gotta go. You'll probably be okay. Lock your bedroom door, if you can. See you tomorrow. Then we can decide what to do about . . . all this."

Of course my bedroom door didn't lock. I considered pushing the bureau in front of it, but Mom and Dad would hear and then I'd be back to the clinic again. But how was I going to sleep, knowing that Julian had been in my room already? I couldn't sleep over at somebody else's house at such late notice, especially on a school night. I'd probably be up all night, afraid to close my eyes for a second.

I checked the house from top to bottom, not worrying about Mom and Dad, who exchanged looks. What I was worrying about was the fact that I had to walk Chang. If I told them I was afraid to do that, I'd *really* be back at the clinic again.

And even though I knew logically that I probably really was in danger, and felt scared, for some reason I was nevertheless itching to get outside.

Chang didn't need a leash; he would never run away. "This is going to be a really quick walk," I said as we went out the door, which I made sure to lock behind me. We went down the three steps to the sidewalk. "Hurry up and do your stuff and we'll go back in before—"

Everything went black.

5

And stayed black.

I was glad about that. I didn't want to see where I was. The way it smelled and felt here was so unspeakably disgusting that if I could see, too, I knew I would throw up or pass out.

What felt like chewed-up bits of half-digested fishy food surged around me, squishing against my skin. A salty thickish liquid like blood flooded past, and also tides of something stinging and acidic. I gagged, and clung desperately to something like a soft and slimy wall so I wouldn't be swept away by the current.

"Welcome, Barney," said Julian's voice, very close to me.

I groaned. "Where . . . am I?" I barely managed to say.

"In my home, the intestine of my host, a very large reptilian thing with a pea-sized brain that's imprisoned on my ship. This is where I *really* am, all the time—what

39

you see of me outside is only a kind of projection. I eat when my host eats, and it's eating now. Mmmm! This is *yummy!*"

This wasn't my imagination, like when we'd played the game this afternoon. This was really happening. I was going to barf. "But . . . why did you bring *me* here?"

"I had to get you alone—and in no position to argue."

I wasn't. All I wanted was out. "What do you want? I'll do it! Just get me out of here! But . . . how can you talk while you're eating?"

"I don't eat with my mouth. I absorb food through my skin. I'm like an intestine turned inside out. I'm attached to my host's intestine with the hooks on my head and—"

Why had I even asked? The gooey, acrid gunk flowed in peristaltic waves all around us. But Julian seemed to have placed me near a small pocket of air so that I could breathe, and talk. "Just get me out of here!" I begged him again.

"I traced The Piggy to this planet. Then saw your helpful Web notice. I know you were the last creature left here who had contact with it. What happened to it?"

Finally he had come out with it. I was relieved that this was all he wanted. Now he'd go chasing after The Piggy and leave me alone, like the others had.

As awful as they had turned out to be, they had never put me through anything like this.

"The lichen got it," I quickly told him. "They were probably flying back to Mbridlengile. Zulma, Moyna, and Jrlb followed them, but the lichen got a head start—and the others aren't immune to them. Go after the lichen. And *get me out of here!*"

"Not so fast, my friend. Why didn't the lichen eat *you?*"

"I was immune. I took a pill."

"*Immune?* The lichen have The Piggy and *you* have *lichen immunity?*" I had never heard him sound so excited, even when he was winning the board game.

"Yeah, but the immunity seemed to go away after a while." I clung to the wall, struggling to keep my head above the loathsome mush surging around me. "They bit my toenails when they left."

"That lichen immunity is permanent. They can never eat you. They nibbled your toenails, not your flesh, right? Because of that pill, you yourself will always be as disgusting to them as this place is to you. This is . . . *phenomenal!* More than I ever dared to hope for. It would be so incredibly helpful to me to have a creature with lichen immunity on my side. Not to mention, Mbridlengile is very, very far away. The lichen will need to make a rest stop. My guess is J'koot—they're comfortable there, and most other gaming species aren't."

The slime was sticking to me now. I was making a continuous, concentrated effort not to throw up. I was beginning to slip down the intestinal wall, so I had to desperately kick my feet and cling to what must be Julian's slippery snakelike body so I wouldn't be pulled away by the powerful waves of stinking bodily fluids all around us—I didn't have hooks on my head like Julian did.

"J'koot," I gasped. "But that's—that's the planet with the crab things who torture and eat people."

"But also, as you agreed, J'koot is very beautiful, and uniquely comfortable to humans—if you can avoid the crabs. Wouldn't you like a little trip there?"

41

And—inexplicably—I *did*. I wanted to go to J'koot like I'd never wanted anything before in my life. I couldn't understand it.

I was slipping down again. Some of the hideous reeking gunk lapped against my lips. "And . . . I'll *die* if I have to stay in here a second longer!" I screamed at him. "And then I won't be useful to you at all!"

"Go and bathe."

And then I was out of there.

But not on the sidewalk in front of our house. I lay dripping on a metal floor.

And beside me, in a cage, a very large reptile roared.

The roaring was worse than anything in a dinosaur movie, wet and guttural and alive.

Julian had said he lived inside the intestine of a large reptile imprisoned on his ship. There was a towering dinosaur, there was a cage that barely held it, and around me, packed into the small space left, were all kinds of complicated equipment.

Was I on Julian's ship, headed for J'koot? Where else *could* I be?

Julian must have beamed me up here, first into his intestinal home, and now out of it. He had waited until I went out to walk Chang—I remembered from the summer that you could only be beamed up to a ship when you were outside.

Now I was terrified at just *being* here. The other aliens

hadn't ever taken me to their ships. Were we out of Earth orbit yet? What if . . .

In the next instant I felt calmer. I didn't understand why, but I was glad. I took a good look around.

This place wasn't sleek and shiny and huge like the spaceships on movies and TV. It seemed to be only one room, and the walls and ceiling were all creaky, complicated gadgets, with wires, that looked more mechanical than electronic. Everything was grimy or streaked with black grease or green slime, as if the place had never once been cleaned. The pervasive stench would have seemed unbearable to me if I hadn't just come from a place that smelled even worse.

Mainly, it contained the huge cage. And inside the cage raged the tremendous dinosaur.

It wasn't happy. It seemed hungry, shaking the cage with its tiny clawed forearms, bellowing. Julian hadn't had enough to eat yet.

And the three robots knew it. They were clunky, rusted things with four legs and two arms and square heads with no mouths and one huge lens. They were engaged in a sort of bucket brigade. One stood near a huge vat of liquid, which must be where the briny smell was coming from. It dipped in a bucket and passed it to the robot in the middle, who hefted it up to the third robot, standing on a ladder just outside the cage. It dumped the contents of the bucket into the reptile's gaping maw. Out of the bucket flowed wriggling shrimplike creatures, just like the stuff that had flowed past me when I was inside the intestine with Julian. I gagged at the memory.

How was I going to clean up? I had to get out of these disgusting clothes.

But at least the roaring stopped. The feeding went on. I tried not to think about the slimy worm within the reptile's body, absorbing the chewed-up food through its skin, an inside-out intestine itself. But I couldn't not think about it. At least I didn't have to worry about what *I* was going to eat; at this moment I felt like I never wanted to eat again in my life.

Finally the reptile calmed down and the feeding stopped. The robots, ignoring me completely, began fussing around with the gadgets on the walls. There was no chair or anything remotely like something for me to sit on.

Julian's voice, issuing a command in some strange language, came out of the dinosaur's mouth. And then Julian appeared beside me. Now I knew why he looked fuzzy. He wasn't really there, he was inside the dinosaur. Unlike the aliens last summer, his human disguise was only a projection.

He gazed admiringly at the reptile, which was now curled in the muck on the floor of its cage, its heavy-lidded eyes half-closed. "Lovely bloke, though he does get a little restive at times," Julian said fondly. "He'd be even bigger if I wasn't in there, and wouldn't need to be fed so often. As it is, he stays just the right size for this ship." He yawned. "I could use a nap right now, after my lunch, so I'm going to cut off this projection. You'll have to entertain yourself, somehow."

"But . . . do the robots know where to go?"

"They've already programmed the ship to head for J'koot."

My heart jumped with excitement at that. The part of me that was still rational said, "How can you be sure the lichen and The Piggy are on J'koot?"

"The lichen have several months' head start on us, lad. No way to follow their ship directly. J'koot's their most likely resting place. If the lichen aren't there, then we can make a new plan. Now I *must* have my nap."

"Wait!" I screamed. "Is there a bathroom? I have to clean off this . . . stuff."

"The compartment to the left of the view screen, with a crescent moon painted on it. An Earth custom, so I hear. I don't use it, of course. My host—he's a pic-theosaur—just does it wherever he happens to be. My robots clean it up for me."

Not often enough, I wanted to tell him.

"The bathroom is pretty standard, adaptable for most species. Sorry there's no entertainment center here. I don't need it. You'll have to be clever and find some way to fill up your time." And he blinked away before telling me exactly how *much* time I was going to have to fill up in this fish-reeking comfortless cramped space.

The bathroom cubicle was a little bigger than an airplane toilet, but nowhere near as comfortable. The toilet was a lidless basin you had to squat over—probably most species didn't sit up when they went to the bathroom—and it was just on the verge of being too big for me to use without falling in.

To the left of the toilet was something like a drain on the floor, and holes in the ceiling above it. Eventually I found the right button and smelly lukewarm water sprayed down on me. I took off my soggy clothes and held them under the water—remembering just in time about the slim volume of poetry from English class in my jacket pocket. I threw it out the bathroom door and continued rinsing off my clothes and myself, pushing the button over and over again, until I finally felt almost decent.

I was uncomfortable about walking around the ship naked, but then decided it didn't matter. Who was there to see me but a dinosaur and some robots? I took my dripping clothes as far away from the putrid cage as I could get them, and managed to hang them up on gadgets on the wall. The robots didn't stop me, so I figured the clothes weren't interfering with any important equipment.

And I wondered again how long I was going to be in this place. It would have been nice if Julian had told me.

Then I remembered the poetry book. Studying seemed pointless, since I had no idea when I'd be back at school again. But it was better than nothing. And it would distract me from worrying about what Mom and Dad were doing right now—they must have noticed I hadn't come back from walking Chang.

There was one bare space on a wall and I sat down on the floor and leaned back with the book. The robots were ignoring me completely, which was comforting. Perhaps they were used to Julian whisking other creatures off with him.

And then a terrible thought struck me: What reason did Julian have for whisking me *back* to Earth? No reason at all. How was I ever going to get home again?

I probably wasn't.

Why hadn't I worried about that before? And why wasn't I worrying about it a whole lot more now? I felt disgusted, but a whole lot calmer than I would ever have expected to feel in this situation. It was spooky.

I opened the book to a poem by Yeats, "The Song of Wandering Aengus."

Barney was now on his way to exactly the place where Madame Toxoplasma Gondii wanted him to go—the place *she* had to get to in order to complete her natural life cycle. If she had been a less practical and determined creature, she might have taken some time off to pat herself on the back for arranging things so cleverly. But that was not her way.

She was working hard, carefully mixing and pumping hormones into Barney's bloodstream to prevent him from being hysterical and afraid. If he was hysterical he might hurt himself, and that would be very bad for her, at this point in her life. And if he was afraid, that could prevent her from reaching her permanent home, the next step in her natural evolution. Barney had to get to J'koot safely, and he had to *not* be too afraid. He would certainly be a bit afraid no matter what she did; that was human nature, she knew. But if she were diligent enough, and able to manufacture enough of her special hormones in exactly the right proportions, and to fill Barney with them, then he would be a lot more willing to take risks on J'koot—and her survival depended upon Barney taking risks.

She took a short break to look out through his eye. He was reading a poem about someone spending his life searching the world for the woman he loved.

Love! That was one of the things about humans that Madame Gundil could not understand. Procreation, reproduction, yes, these were essential for her, too. It was the necessity for offspring that was driving her to J'koot; she could only have her babies there.

But this thing about love, about caring only for one other individual, was beyond her comprehension. Especially baffling was the concept of sacrifice, of giving things up, and taking risks, and making compromises, in order to *help* the individual one loved. Why did humans waste their time in that foolish way? How could they give up things that *they* wanted just to help another? Baffling, baffling.

But she couldn't sit around wasting her time trying to understand this peculiar species. She had waited long enough for the supply of hormones to build up again, and now she had to continue mixing them in the proper doses and feeding them to Barney.

Because it would take a lot of exactly the right hormones, over a long period of time, to make him calm enough not to be too afraid of the crabs.

8

An hour or so later I was interrupted from my reading by a belch from the dinosaur.

I looked up from the book.

The dinosaur reared its head and clawed at the air and out of its mouth came Julian's voice. "How's everything going, Barney?"

I didn't like talking to the dinosaur. "Can't you project yourself in human form?" I asked him. "It's kind of easier for me to deal with you that way."

"Yes, but it takes a lot of effort, and here on the ship, what's the point?" he said. "You know the situation, I don't need to disguise myself anymore. I just appeared in human form before to kind of acclimate you. Of course I can't see anything from in here unless I activate the projection, but why do I need to see? Just speak up and don't mumble, there's a good chap."

He paused, and the dinosaur wriggled in the muck on the floor of its cage. "Funnily enough, you don't sound as if you're dying of boredom—or panicking either."

"I don't know why I'm not panicking," I told him. "But the reason I'm not bored is that I have a book."

"Good for you. Now I don't have to worry about you entertaining yourself."

I didn't really believe he had spent a lot of time worrying about that.

The dinosaur swiveled its head around and roared. When it finished, I said, "Yeah, but . . ." I was hesitant to mention this, but I had no choice. "I *am* worried about how I'm going to get back home. *That's* what's bothering me."

"All in good time, Barney, my boy." The voice echoed a little from inside the dinosaur's body. "No question of going back to Earth until I get The Piggy, of course. Then we'll think about it. It all depends on strategy. Can't let the others know I'm going back there, can we? Then they'd all be after me."

That set me thinking. Was it possible that I might be able to outwit them all again? To get control of a ship and learn how to use it and fly back to Earth? *I* didn't care about getting The Piggy.

I had figured out pretty much for sure that the game was a fake and The Piggy was only a recording device that did *not* blow up planets. It was fooling the aliens. Once they got to wherever The Piggy was, they would care only about The Piggy, not me. If I ran away without The Piggy, what reason would they have to chase me?

"Well, you can't expect me not to want to go home again," I said.

The dinosaur only farted in response.

Then there was a crackling sound from the ship's equipment, followed by a scratchy, high-pitched voice babbling way too fast, like a roaring rooster on fast-forward. I jerked, suddenly frightened again.

"Sorry, my friend. Can't understand a word you're saying. We're going to have to use English as our common language, I'm afraid," said the worm inside the dinosaur as the dinosaur rolled over in the muck.

"Well, I guess it doesn't matter if the two human larvae can understand us," drawled a deep, vibrating female voice. "We're not going to mouth each other the truth anyway." The speaker chuckled deeply.

Two human larvae? Did that mean there was another human with this creature that was contacting us? Katie had said Matt followed her home, acting very peculiar. Was it possible that *Matt* was another alien, and had abducted her, too? Did I dare to hope I wasn't alone in this situation?

"Who is that?" I asked the dinosaur. "Is it someone in another ship?" And then, without waiting for an answer, I shouted in the direction the voice was coming from, "Katie! Are you there? Are you okay?"

"I'm here, Barney!" came Katie's voice. "Matt grabbed me. But Matt's not . . . he's . . . she's an alien. But I'm okay . . . I guess."

The joy I felt at knowing she was in contact with us, and safe, was stronger than any of the peculiar emotions that had been flooding through me recently.

"Silence! We can't waste our precious ansible time on your piddling!" the female voice commanded. Matt must have assumed his true alien form, and it was fe-

male, just as Manny had been a male human but a female alien named Moyna. For Katie's sake, I hoped
Matt's alien form wasn't too disgusting. "Guanophilia!"
she barked. "I have sensors that noted the presence of
any interstellar ships in orbit around that nothing little
planet we just departed. You and I were the only such
ships. As soon as the electronic ears and eyes sensed you
leaving, I snatched up my human female lure, my slave,
my organic bauble, and followed you. I have done my
research. J'koot is a convenient resting place for the
lichen. That means you must believe the lichen have
The Piggy. Is that your reasoning, Guanophilia?"

"Blimey! I'm so flattered that you know my name,"
Julian said evasively. "However did you find out who
I am?"

"From the game, idiot. And the human larva spewed
out more about you under questioning," the woman
said, and I worried about what the "questioning" had
been like for Katie. "Don't worm out of my request,
worm. What is your reason for going to J'koot?"

"You must have suspected that Barney was the last human to see The Piggy, as I did, or you wouldn't have
spent so much time with him. As for J'koot—well, Barney was reading about it in the rule book. That's what
brought it to mind." Julian paused. "I'm not sure we're
even going there at all. I have no reason to—"

He was interrupted by a harsh guffaw. "Don't test that
with me. I've already measured your coordinates. You're
headed directly for J'koot. You must intuit the lichen
have The Piggy on J'koot, whether you'll cough it up
or not."

The dinosaur actually slurped up some of the excrement in its cage. "Don't forget, wherever The Piggy may be, the others will be there—the spider, the gas bag, and the fish," it said, not mentioning the lichen one way or the other. "We'll have them to contend with, too. I reckon it might be to our advantage to make some sort of deal with each other," Julian's voice suggested. "If we work together, we might be able to outwit all the rest. You must be a new player, or you would have picked your own card in the board game, like Barney and me. What are you, anyway?"

"The closest English word to it is *wasp*. Copidosoma, to be explicit," she said, sounding a bit proud. "You may address me as Soma for short."

Matt's large glasses *had* made him look rather insect-like. I wondered how big the wasp woman was. Poor Katie!

"Spot on!" Julian said, sounding excited. "You're the ones who use your ovipositors to lay your eggs inside a living host, and your little darlings grow by eating its living flesh from the inside, leaving the vital organs alone until the very end so the host will stay alive—in agony—for as long as possible. How clever your babies are! A bit brutal, but clever nonetheless."

"Thank you," she said complacently. "My last brood counted 2,018 females and one male. The simian host went on living—if you can call it that—for a month before they all came bursting out of it. Glorious! Glorious!"

"Not humans!" I shouted. "You wouldn't use a human host, would you?"

"I've never sampled," she said. "But it might just be tasty, don't you think?"

"Katie, don't let her!" I yelled. "Keep away from the ovipositor!"

Soma and Julian both laughed now as the dinosaur continued to eat its feces. "Don't breathe so naive, Barney," Soma said. "She couldn't prevent me. Lucky for her I've laid a brood recently and it's not my time again yet. We'll observe what happens later on. Guanophilia! What's your host?"

"My host is a pictheosaurus from the planet Voeves. Quite large and a good fighter. How about you?"

"I'm just a trifle bigger than the average human—and I bear a wicked sting, too."

What would it feel like to be stung by a human-sized wasp?

"Splendid." Julian paused, and then said in a lilting voice as the dinosaur wiped more excrement over its face with a claw, "I don't suppose you'd care to tell me what attributes and devices you have."

Soma laughed again. "Conniving a deal to eat together for a time is one thing," she said. "Giving away what attributes and weapons I possess is another thing altogether. I've digested that much about the game already."

"Yes, well, I have my little secrets, too," he said, and I knew he was referring to my immunity to the lichen. That would put him at a huge advantage over all the other players, since they were all terrified of any contact with the lichen—who could eat anything alive—and I could just walk right through them unharmed to The

Piggy. Luckily Katie didn't know I was immune, or the wasp woman might have gotten it out of her by "questioning."

"Now, Soma," Julian went on. "What say we rendezvous in orbit around J'koot? Check the place out. See what we can see before beaming down to the surface, just to be on the safe side. Our first objective will be to find out who has The Piggy, and then get rid of the others. We can work together on that. Then we'll see who gets The Piggy." He still wasn't admitting that he knew the lichen had The Piggy, even though Soma had figured it out already.

"You have a hidden reason to snatch Barney, any idiot can observe that," Soma said. "Since I am an infant at playing the real game, I waited and watched to see what you would do. Then I took Katie. *My* advantage consists that I have her. Protecting her from my ovipositor would be a powerful control over Barney, I'd say—maybe even enough to prevent him from doing what *you* want."

"We'll see," Julian said. "First we get rid of the others. Barney can tell me what attributes they have. We'll meet in orbit." Then they started talking coordinates, which I didn't understand.

At least Katie was safe, so far. But she seemed to be in worse danger than I was. Julian's host wasn't in pain and Julian didn't want it to die. He even called it a lovely bloke. As much as I'd prefer not to, I *could* survive with a tapeworm in my gut.

But if Soma laid her eggs inside Katie, she'd die in slow agony as they ate her flesh in order to grow. Soma was right. I would do a lot to prevent that.

"Righty-oh! See you then," Julian said brightly as the dinosaur stuck out its tongue and licked the muck around its mouth. "Bye-eee." One of the robots flipped a switch and the hum of the communication was cut off.

"Well, now we have a nice little party to look forward to," Julian said. "A wasp, a dinosaur, three robots, and two human teenagers—not to mention whatever other slaves the wasp might have working for her." The dinosaur lumbered to its feet again and swung its tail.

"Is it possible to see out of this ship?" I asked him.

"There's an adjustable telescopic view screen opposite the front of my cage," he said. "You could kill some time taking a look, though you won't see much at FTL."

Of course I knew FTL meant faster than light. "How can you talk to another ship when you're both going FTL?" I asked him. "I didn't think that was possible."

"Luckily we both have special ansibles for that. Not all ships have them yet."

"So how long is it going to take us to get there?"

"Let me think on that a moment . . ." he said, taking his time on purpose, I was sure.

I dreaded the answer. How long could I stand to be stuck in this smelly, cramped place? As disgusted as I still felt, I knew I was going to have to eat sometime. But not the stuff they fed the dinosaur! I'd starve to death before eating that.

"Of course, it doesn't matter to me *how* long it takes, I'm as comfortable as I can be," Julian went on, continuing to prolong his answer. The dinosaur splashed the muck with its tail. "But we *are* going as fast as we can, because the others are so many months ahead of us. Still, the lichen do need a certain amount of time on J'koot to replenish their stores of slime mold. And I think The Piggy's pretty safe with them, since the others don't have immunity, and the lichen are tough little critters. You had a little taste of the pain they can inflict, so you said."

I sighed with impatience. I was getting used to talking to the dinosaur now, so I was less scared of showing my real emotions. "Yeah, but how long is it going to take?" I asked him again, irritably. "And how am I going to eat, and stuff like that?"

"Oh, don't worry about those little things. You've already familiarized yourself with the bathroom. Certainly it's not as comfortable for you as one designed specifically for humans would be, but you can use it. The food will taste a bit strange, but you can eat it. You will survive."

"Yeah, but for *how long?*"

"No need to get touchy about it, my lad."

I got up and stalked over to the view screen. It showed nothing but a murky blur. Some way to kill time! I was furious at the way Julian was teasing me, refusing to answer my question, but I still wasn't at ease enough to actually get angry at him.

And then he relented. "You're in luck, my lad," he said. "Only a week and a half, by your reckoning."

"But it'll be a lot longer than that at home, won't it?" I said.

"I don't feel like talking about that now. I want another nap." He sure took naps a lot. Still, what else was there for him to do in there? "But don't worry. If you ever get home, it's possible that you may see your parents again."

My heart sank. I was in a much worse mess than I had even realized.

On movies and TV, space travel was portrayed as an exciting adventure. In reality it was inconvenient beyond belief, because of the time dilation aspect. The closer you got to the speed of light—and we were going *beyond* it—the slower time went for you, relative to the rest of the universe. I had read about the famous twin paradox, in which one twenty-four-year-old twin travels in a spaceship at 99 percent of the speed of light, and the other twenty-four-year-old twin stays home on Earth. When the astronaut twin returns, his earthbound twin is eighty-four years old and the astronaut is twenty-six. That was going to happen to me in relation to everyone I knew.

Even so, I was still more eager than ever to get to J'koot.

I spent the week and a half brooding and reading and having occasional chats with Julian. Mostly the chats consisted of Julian grilling me about the aliens I had met last summer, and their attributes. I tried to ask him questions, too, but he was cagey, of course, and I didn't learn any more from him about J'koot or his real plans than I had learned from his conversation with the wasp. And he wouldn't let me talk to Katie on his ansible, no matter how much I begged him. He said the ansible ate up a huge amount of energy at this speed, and could only be used for essentials.

Not that Katie and I could have made any plans with the two of them listening anyway.

Only once, during the whole trip, did the robots clean out the dinosaur's cage. They shoveled up the gunk and dumped it into a metallic-looking bag, which sealed automatically shut. They opened a round hatch in the wall, put the bag in, closed the hatch, and pushed a button. A red light blinked briefly.

"What did they do with that stuff?" I asked Julian.

"Put it in the garbage disposal," he said. "It shoots the garbage out of the ship. At FTL speed. But it also does a lot more. Pretty nifty little device. It keeps the garbage hidden so it won't be an eyesore to anything. It also keeps it automatically as far away as possible from any inhabited planets, and any ships, and in fact anyplace where there's any life at all. Don't want to be a litterbug now, do we?"

"Nice of you to be so thoughtful," I muttered, wishing he were less of a litterbug on his own ship.

I also kept my eyes on what else the robots were doing, trying to figure out how they operated the ship, just in case we might ever have a chance to escape in it. The problem was, I could not get my mind to make logical sense of what the robots were doing. I couldn't even tell what was different about their behavior when the week and a half was over and we reached the orbit of J'koot.

Slowing down from FTL gave you a peculiar sensation in the gut, but I could deal with it. And it was interesting to watch the blur on the view screen dissolve and fizzle and then become a green planet with a gorgeous glow of atmosphere around it. At the sight of it my heart jumped with longing. J'koot!

We docked with Soma the wasp's ship, which involved a lot of running around by the robots and some tricky maneuvering, but finally there was a satisfying crunch and we stabilized. We needed one final conference before going down to the planet. Since the dinosaur didn't have much of a brain and had to be confined to its cage, it was decided that Soma and Katie would come over to our ship. "*I* have nothing to hide," Julian said brightly.

There was obviously some kind of universal connecting chamber for these ships. A round door opened like a camera lens, and in walked a great big red thing and behind it—Katie! I didn't bother to take a good look at Soma yet. Katie and I ran together. We had never even held hands before, but now we clung to each other. We were both even crying a little bit, a mixture of happiness and other emotions, too. "Oh, Barney! I was afraid I'd never see you again."

"Me, too! I'm so sorry I got you into this mess. But I'm so glad you're here!" I was sure she didn't know about FTL travel and time dilation. At some point I was going to have to break the news to her that everyone we knew on Earth might already be dead. But now wasn't the time.

"I don't know what I'd do if anything happened to you," she said, still holding on to me. Then she stepped back. "But Barney. Why didn't you tell me the game was real?"

"Would you have believed me? Or thought I was crazy?"

"Enough of this pathetic human emotional regurgitation," said Soma's deep voice. "Let's get down to the task. My God, the stench in here is revolting!"

Katie wrinkled her nose. "Barney, how could you stand it for all that time?"

I shrugged. "I got used to it, I guess. And after being inside that intestine, *nothing* will ever seem disgusting to me again."

"Intestine?" Katie said.

"Julian lives in that thing's intestine," I told her, gesturing at the huge dinosaur. "When he first beamed me up to his ship he brought me in there with him." I lowered my voice. "It was the worst thing that ever happened to me. I . . . I keep being afraid he might do it again."

Katie visibly shuddered. "Oh, Barney," she said.

Now I took a better look at Soma. She was pretty alarming, but nothing as gross as Moyna, the gas bag. She was about seven feet tall, a rusty color, and segmented, with a big round head, a swollen abdomen, and six sticklike legs. She had two huge multifaceted eyes and two antennae, and two gossamer wings. The foot-long ovipositor that protruded from her abdomen was needle sharp. It was impossible not to think of the horror it could inflict.

She didn't seem to be wearing any breathing apparatus either. "You breathe air, too?" I asked her.

"A lucky stroke for all of us. What breathe the others you befriended?"

Julian already knew this, of course. I glanced at the dinosaur. "Go ahead, Barney. She'll find out anyway," Julian said.

"When they were disguised as humans you couldn't see their breathing apparatus, but they all needed it. So they'll be at a disadvantage on J'koot."

Soma glanced at the dinosaur. "You must have amputated a wealth of information from him," she said dryly. "I wonder how much you'll allow him to share with me?"

"He knows what he can tell and what he can't," Julian said, and his voice was not jovial at all. It was like steel, as the dinosaur lolled on its back, its two fore claws on its fat belly. "He knows where I can put him if he betrays me."

I knew he was warning me not to mention my lichen immunity. The wasp would do anything to get control of me if she knew about it—and she could do some very terrible things. I felt sick again. The immunity protected me, yes. But it also made me the prize all the others would want. I would have infinitely preferred to be useless, and ignored.

Would the aliens from the summer remember that I was immune?

Then I thought of something. "Hey, maybe they got old," I said suddenly. "I mean if years went by on Earth while we were traveling here, that means . . ." And then I was struck by a huge discrepancy. "Wait a minute," I said. "If years went by on Earth while we were traveling here, because of time dilation, then how come years didn't go by for *us* on Earth while *they* were traveling here?"

Soma sighed, as if it were a dumb question. Julian was more patient. "FTL changes everything, Barney," he said. "Yes, if we were crawling along at 99 percent of the speed of light, then time dilation would be in effect and years would be rushing by on Earth. But once you get past the light barrier and go *faster* than light—which your poor scientists still think is impossible—then everything changes. It evens out. Time stays the same for both. When I said your parents might still be alive, I wasn't referring to time dilation. I was referring to how long our business here might possibly take."

"What are you talking about?" Katie asked.

"I'll explain later," I told her. "It just means we're a whole lot luckier than I thought. If we ever get back, things might still be pretty much the same." It was a huge relief to know that.

Not that there was much chance we'd ever get back.

"Can we please cling to the important things?" Soma said irritably. She took a step closer, her multifaceted eyes on me. "I am very hungry to know what is Barney's special attribute. If he doesn't cough it up soon, then I may feel the craving to have some more babies—perhaps in a human host."

"No!" I screamed, starting toward Katie. The wasp barred my way, thrusting out her ovipositor.

"I thought you said it wasn't your time yet, my dear," Julian reminded her.

She buzzed with annoyance. "But it will be soon," she snapped. "And my threat is very real." She stepped back again, and seemed to be trying to calm down a little. "Meanwhile, what about the others? If our first goal is to extinguish the other species who want The Piggy, then the more we *all* know about them the more successful we'll be."

"Go ahead, Barney. Tell her what you know. But *only* about the other species." The dinosaur gurgled and drool spouted out of its mouth.

I told her how Jrlb had the hyperspace card, Zulma

had the brain booster, and Moyna had the youth serum. I told her about Jrlb's sword, his lasso, his glasses to see in the dark, and the various blasters, and how Zulma could spit acidlike venom and tie you up in her threads in seconds. In the end, she knew everything about the aliens that Julian did.

"Do you have equipment to observe the surface from this stinking tub?" Soma wanted to know.

"Please don't talk that way about my home," Julian said defensively. "I have all the latest equipment. I just don't waste time and effort on what some species refer to as 'aesthetics.' What I consider to be comfortable is a little . . . different, as Barney well knows. The viewer is right opposite the front of the cage. I'm sure you know how to operate it."

"And it has a porcine locator?"

"To a range of a few kilometers—nothing can pinpoint it any closer than that."

"Well, here comes the big moment," Soma muttered. "The Piggy better be here or I'll become quite violent." She lumbered over to the viewer and began pressing buttons with her left foreleg. The globe grew in size and then various features—mountain ranges, oceans, cities— flashed past so quickly you could hardly see them. I was dying to see more! But suddenly the screen showed the distant globe again.

"No sign of it!" Soma snarled, turning threateningly back to us.

"There's another hemisphere, you know," Julian said sarcastically. "We have to go around to the other side to get it in range. We can do it while we're still locked— it'll only take half an hour."

"I think Katie and I will choose to spend that time in a more aesthetic—as you put it—environment, then," Soma said. "Come, Katie dear. And don't gulp down any ideas about being alone with your little friend."

The dinosaur burped cavernously.

We sped around to the other side of the planet. I stood watching at the viewing screen, longing more than ever to get down there. Katie and I would just have to be careful of the crabs, that's all.

When we stopped, Soma and Katie didn't come back. "She's looking on her own, the bloody lying cheat—and after I allowed you to give her all that information. Run across to her ship, Barney, and see what the porcine locator's telling her. And don't say a *word* about you-know-what." He barked an order in another language and the robots hurried through the lenslike opening. I followed them.

Now, *this* was more like what you'd expect a spaceship to be like. Soma was a tidier housekeeper than Julian— or at any rate her antlike robots were. Every surface gleamed, and there was no stench and no piles of excrement. Her robots were smaller than Julian's, around six inches tall, and there were about a dozen of them. At the moment they were lined up against one wall like shoes in a closet.

There were no human-style chairs here, but the wiring was not exposed, and everything was smooth and gently curved, with no sharp angles. The arrays of colored lights were works of art. Instead of screens like computer terminals, information floated out from the silver walls in three dimensions, in symbols I could not understand. I couldn't help feeling a *bit* envious that Katie had spent all this time in an environment so much pleasanter than mine.

The viewer was not a screen. It was also a three-dimensional display, and as I entered I could see the features of J'koot's other hemisphere zooming past—oceans, mountains, and especially intriguing cities and villages. Only this time it did not return to the view of the globe. It zeroed in on a jungle. A red light blinked there: the porcine locator. It must indicate that The Piggy was in the jungle. But the locator could pinpoint only The Piggy, it seemed, and not other creatures. The canopy of foliage hid the lichen—if they were the ones who had The Piggy—and whatever other species might be in the area.

Soma wasn't using a keyboard, she was manipulating symbols floating in the air as she watched the display, and murmuring to herself in what must have been her own buzzing snarl of a language.

Julian's robots were also watching the display and Soma's symbols, no doubt conveying the information back to him.

Probably we'd soon be going down to the jungle. I ached with disappointment. I wanted to go to the cities.

That was how I felt, but I was still bewildered by it. *Why* did I want to go to the cities, where the crabs obviously lived, and where I'd be much more likely to be eaten by them? It was baffling.

Soma was busy with her work. Katie turned as I approached. I put a finger to my lips, and then beckoned with it. She came back with me to the connecting point between the ships, as far as we could get from both Soma and Julian.

"We don't have much time," I whispered. "Could you operate this ship if we had the chance? I don't have a clue how to fly Julian's, even though I watched the robots a lot."

To my surprise, Katie nodded. "I watched, too. Especially how she communicated with the robots. It was like—she found J'koot on a map, and then they did all the rest. If I could just find a picture of Earth on the same map, I think it might be possible for me to get them to take the ship back home—if they'd obey anybody but her, I mean."

That was amazingly wonderful news. So why wasn't I more excited? Was it because Katie had figured out something that I hadn't? But had I even really tried?

Of course I didn't say any of that to her. "Great!" I whispered, and gave Katie a silent thumbs-up gesture, and then we returned to the view of J'koot, before Soma or Julian's robots noticed we'd had a secret conference.

Soma was still busy; she didn't seem to be aware we'd been off by ourselves. So I asked her the first logical question that came to my mind. "Okay, so The Piggy's there, right? Are there any other ships in orbit?"

"Three," she said, without turning away from her work. "Let's hope they belong to your three friends. We know something about them, at least. If it is them, they've been in orbit here for months."

"But shouldn't there be four ships?" I said, without thinking. Then I snapped my mouth shut. I shouldn't have said that. I didn't want to even *remind* her that the lichen existed.

She turned and gave me a long stare. "Would you be

referring to the lichen? If they're still around, they must have landed. They need to replenish their stores of slime mold. And my computer tells me that the jungles of J'koot are a good place for that." She stared at me for another moment, thinking, as I stood there starting to sweat. Would she figure it out?

Finally she shook her head and turned away. "Don't bother me, I'm working. And why should I give away any more information to you anyway?"

"But I told you a lot!" I argued.

She made a brittle rasping noise that might have been a laugh. "While I was on your planet I learned that your species has at least one partially sensible saying, something about how you can get away with anything when you're at war. And this is war."

"'All's fair in love and war,'" I said, thinking how natural it was that she would forget the love part. To her, the act of "love" meant agonizing death to another.

"Now my eyes tell me exactly where it is," Soma said. "The three of us can beam down and see what's happening."

"Hey, what about Julian?" I said.

"Who needs *him*?" she said.

As much as I wanted to get to J'koot as soon as possible, I still felt a certain loyalty to Julian. He hadn't been all that wonderfully kind to me, but at least he pretended to care. And he *did* have a real sense of humor, which this creature didn't. Not to mention his life didn't depend on torturing and killing his host, the way hers did. Disgusting as he was, he was certainly the nicer of the two of them, and I'd prefer to take my chances with him. I took Katie's hand to pull her over to his ship.

But I didn't move fast enough. In a moment Katie and I and Soma were standing in a dark green twilight, full of the sound of dripping water and unrecognizable whispers—the jungle of J'koot.

My heart lifted. I felt literally drugged, I was so happy. This was where I belonged! Now, if only I could get to the nearest crab settlement or village, then I'd have everything I wanted . . .

I shook my head. What was the matter with me? I had to stay *away* from the crabs if I wanted to live much longer. What was this death wish that kept influencing me? It was beginning to seem more dangerous than anything else about the situation.

And the situation was plenty dangerous enough. First of all there were the crabs, to whom Katie and I were marvelous, rare delicacies. I didn't see any in the immediate vicinity, but this was their planet, so they'd be around eventually.

Then there was the fact that The Piggy was nearby.

And wherever The Piggy was, there would be scheming and fighting and mayhem of all kinds. As Zulma the spider lady had explained to me last summer, the gaming species would stop at nothing to get it. One species had it now, and there were at least three others here, too. There were also Soma and Julian.

And then there was my lichen immunity, which would make me the focus of all the species who knew about it. Julian knew. The aliens from last summer might remember, or figure it out if they didn't know already—they weren't stupid. Soma didn't know yet, but she could find out soon.

And she had other weapons besides her ovipositor. *All* the gaming species had weapons, in addition to their own vicious natural attributes. Except for Katie and me, who had nothing. If only I'd at least brought the neural whip I'd used last summer! But of course I hadn't known this was going to happen.

It was hot and very humid here—you could hear water dripping everywhere in the green dimness underneath the dense canopy of foliage. Katie and I were dressed for November. We'd left our coats on the ships, but we still had on the same long pants and long-sleeved heavy shirts we'd been wearing for the past week and a half. Soma had done research about this planet's atmosphere, so she must have known about the climate, too. It would have been nice of her to warn us so we could have left our heavy shirts on the ship and just come down in our T-shirts. But Soma wasn't what you'd call nice.

"Did you have a shower since we left home?" I asked Katie.

"Yes. But it was hard in that stupid bathroom—and there was no soap to wash myself or my clothes. I feel filthy."

"Me, too," I said. I turned to Soma. "We'd like to find a stream or something and get cleaned up. We'd be a lot more comfortable and alert if we could just—"

She laughed. "Not until *after* you've done what I crave you for," she said. "The fresh water on this planet is swarming with flukes and nematodes that will quickly drill their way into your bloodstream and make you totally useless to me. After you've done your job, go ahead and let them feed on you."

Of course she hadn't told us that to help us, but it was good to know.

"Well? What do you want us to do?" Katie asked her.

"Principally I thirst for Barney, for whatever special attribute he has that makes Julian think he can help him get The Piggy. And I thirst for you, Katie dear, as persuasion. If Barney doesn't do exactly what *I* want him to do, out comes the ovipositor."

And certainly there would come a time—probably soon—when what Soma wanted me to do would be different from what Julian wanted. Then it would be a choice between Katie dying a slow painful death and me going into the intestine. Intestine, here I come! I gulped.

The trees were taller than any I'd ever seen on Earth, with huge leaves that blotted out the sky and made the jungle dark green and deeply shadowed. There was little foliage on the ground, only dead leaves, which was comforting in the sense that there were fewer places for crawling things like snakes and weird insects to hide.

But there were rustlings and chittering chirpings every-where, and movement in the tree branches and foliage. I could see the movement out of the corner of my eye, but whenever I turned to try to see exactly what was moving, it had vanished.

"The creatures here seem pretty shy," I said.

"That's not exactly the word I'd utter for them, Bar-ney," Soma said. "Sneaky is more like it. When they pounce, they want it to be a surprise."

"So where are your weapons?" I asked her. "You have to protect us if you want us to do your little job for you."

"You know what my major weapon is. The others are hidden. Time for us to get moving. The Piggy is within a radius of one hundred meters or so. We must find and destroy whatever species has it."

"But wouldn't we be safer if Julian was here, too? To use *his* weapons to protect us from the others, too?"

"But then he'd hunger for The Piggy. Come on, this way."

"Of course I want The Piggy," Julian said behind us. We spun around.

It was Julian's voice, but the projection was shockingly different. The thing was about three feet high and had a mottled and stained greenish shell. It had segmented arms at the ends of which were two huge claws, each about two feet long, that had serrated edges and looked very sharp. It waddled toward us, its two pinkish eyes wobbling at the tops of threadlike stalks.

Katie backed away from it, her fist at her mouth. I just stood there staring, repelled but also fascinated.

"Is this supposed to be some sort of a joke?" Soma

76

barked. She sounded angry, but I suspected there might also be a note of fear in her voice.

"Protective coloration, mates," said the crab. "With my projection, I can look like anything I want. So why look like a human, the crabs' most desirable food? This way I won't be so noticeable—and the other gaming species might be a bit put off by me, too."

So *this* was what the crabs looked like. I knew it was really Julian, but I still just stood there staring at it, taking in every detail. It had a very wide, lipless mouth, and when it opened you could see the double rows of razor-sharp teeth, like a shark's.

"Come on! We're shedding time," Soma ordered. She was always impatient. "My sensors tell me it's probably in this direction." She started off through the jungle, quietly, trying to make as little noise as possible on the carpet of leaves. We followed.

What would it be like to see Zulma, Moyna, and Jrlb again, assuming they were here? Certainly they would not be disguised as humans—if they had a choice—for the reason Julian pointed out. Would they be in their true forms, or disguised as something else? Would they be working together or separately?

They would definitely still be angry at me for letting the lichen, who could not be approached or communicated with, get The Piggy in the first place. They would probably kill me for revenge. That would be just like them.

After about ten minutes, Soma, who was in the lead, suddenly stopped. She put a finger to her lips, pointed ahead of her, and then stepped behind a very large tree, its trunk about the diameter of our living room. We followed her as quietly as possible and then peered around the tree.

It was brighter ahead, where she was pointing, a kind of clearing, and there seemed to be something distinctly un-jungle-like in it. Something metallic. We could hear the sound of splashing water. And also voices, speaking in a peculiar but somehow familiar language.

Soma started to step out from behind the tree.

And then the net fell, with hardly a sound at all.

11

After the relative routine of being on the ship—where she only had to feed Barney hormones that made him want to be with the crabs—Madame Gondii now, suddenly, had a tremendous amount of fast work to do.

Much more complicated work.

This planet was her real home, and every cell in her body knew it. This was where she could have her babies. But she had to work hard to make sure Barney didn't ruin everything.

Still, as hard as she had to attend to business, she was also exultant. Getting Barney here was a major victory; it was not the great, final moment, but that would happen next, if she was clever enough. And she wanted it to go smoothly; the sooner the crabs ate him, the better.

Because it had taken Madame Gondii a long time to

reach this planet. Her species was short-lived, and her biological clock was ticking. If she did not have her babies soon, she would be too old to have them at all. And the only place she could have them was inside the body of a crab.

Her natural inclination was to continue what she had been doing, to redouble her efforts to feed Barney even more powerful calming, relaxing hormones. She didn't want him escaping from the crabs, or even making trouble for them.

But it wasn't that simple. She remembered the old adage that had been drilled into her by her mother: *Make the host struggle—or else the crabs will know.*

Her species had evolved over the millennia so that they could only reproduce when inside the body of a crab of J'koot. They took that body over, they made it a sexless robot completely under their control, they modified its reproductive organs so that it would produce Toxoplasma Gondii babies, not crab babies. It was the only way her species could survive.

But unfortunately, the crabs eventually became intelligent. They had learned that any creatures, especially humanoids, who surrendered willingly to them were infected, and would in turn infect other crabs. And that was why Barney had to struggle against them. If he didn't, they would know, and they would burn him instead of eating him, and that would be the end of Madame Gondii and her babies.

And so, even though part of Barney had to want to be with them, and not make any really *serious* attempts to get away, another part of him had to fight them, realistically, so that they would not suspect the presence of Madame Gondii in his brain. He had to be fed conflicting hormones. A complicated recipe indeed.

As the crabs approached the creatures trapped in their net, Madame Gondii labored frantically in her kitchen, pumping out and mixing up stronger and yet more subtle and intricate hormones than ever before. She occasionally peeked out to observe the behavior of Barney's human companion, who served as a model for Barney's behavior, and then rushed back to her equivalent of pots and pans and cookbooks.

And occasionally she allowed herself a glimpse of a crab. All those crabs! She had never seen anything so beautiful in her life. The sight of them made her hungry. So close, so close! And when, oh when, would she get inside one of them?

She hoped they would feast today. She hoped they would eat Barney first.

And she didn't want them to take their time about it, either.

And as she worked, she pondered hard: What could she do to make it happen as fast as possible?

12

We struggled and thrashed, forgetting about being quiet in our terror. But the net was some kind of pliant vine-like mesh, and held us tighter the more we fought it.

And the dozen or so crabs scuttling toward us were not projections.

Again, my heart jumped with excitement.

But at the same time I was shaken, looking at those teeth and claws, thinking of my legs being broken and lying there until they came to amputate . . .

Julian's projection had vanished. Had he blended in with the crabs, or was he safely back on his ship?

The crabs stood around us conversing excitedly in a croaking guttural language, pointing at Katie and me with their claws. How long had it been since a humanoid from one planet or another had come here? How hungry for us were they?

And then, from around the other side of the tree, came my old friends: Zulma, the bulbous, hairy, four-foot-tall spider; Moyna, the floating gas bag with claws, messy with veins and mucus; and Jrlb, the stinking, dripping swordfish man.

Jrlb was holding his breath, so he couldn't talk. But the others could, even in their breathing gear. "Barney, what a wonderful surprise!" cackled Zulma.

"Now you will get your jusst reward!" lisped Moyna.

"Indeed!" Zulma agreed.

Jrlb opened his mouth and water poured out. "Someone brought you here? Of course, he must have lichen immunity!" he gasped. "*I* should have brought him! Now it's too late." He used his hyperspace access to vanish for a breath of water.

Soma glared at me from inside the net, her eyes seeming even bigger than before. She tried to inch toward Katie with her ovipositor.

But by this time the crabs had made the obvious choice. The net was lifted. The crabs ignored the other aliens, moving so fast that Katie and I didn't even have a chance to begin to run. Nor did Soma have time to use her ovipositor. Two crabs grabbed each of us with their two-foot-long sharp serrated claws. They were very strong. There was no escaping them.

I was expecting the claws to tear and scrape my skin. But all I felt was the pressure of their grip. In my excitement and horror I looked down. One crab had me by the arms, the other by the legs. And they were wearing what could only be called gloves on the claws that held me—padded gloves whose obvious purpose was to protect me from being cut. But why were they protecting me from pain?

That couldn't be it. I had read about how brutal and vicious they were. Probably it was just that the skin was tastier if it hadn't been bruised. They wanted their meat perfect and so they handled it carefully, like high-class butchers.

The four crabs carrying us were racing sideways across the forest floor, away from the big tree and the water and whatever had been going on there. They seemed completely indifferent to The Piggy. One part of me felt comfortably cradled, like a baby in its mother's arms. The other part was screaming.

"Help! Julian! Help us!"

Of all the aliens, Julian was the only one who was not almost totally malignant. But unfortunately, he was just a projection here, and couldn't do anything to help us.

But I could hear the footsteps of the other aliens giving chase. They didn't want me to be eaten by the crabs because I could get The Piggy for them. Otherwise they would have been happy to see me die in agony.

Something shot past us, something that looked like an organic syringe—a snakelike body with a tip like a needle at the end of it. An ovipositor arrow? Could Soma actually *shoot* her rapacious eggs at creatures? It bounced harmlessly off the hard shell of a crab in front of us.

More weapons were being fired, too—weapons I remembered the sound of from last summer. But suddenly there was an explosion just behind us. I couldn't see what made it, but the crabs must have weapons, too. After that, the footsteps stopped.

"Katie!" I called out to her. "This is all my fault! I'm sorry, I'm sorry!"

She didn't answer. She was struggling and thrashing violently.

"And I'm sorry you feel the need to apologize, my delicious friend," one of the crabs carrying me said, in gravelly but understandable English. "A great honor is to be bestowed upon the two of you—an honor that is experienced by sadly too few of your species."

I could have pointed out sarcastically that it was not exactly an honor to be maimed and tortured and then cooked and eaten, but the part of me that was afraid didn't have the nerve to say it like that. But I did want to say something, to find out if there was any logic in its brain at all. "We know you're going to eat us," I said, and moaned. "Nobody wants to be eaten. It's horrible!"

"But you do not understand what the honor and the preparation entail," it told me. "I think you will be pleasantly surprised. And . . . er . . ." Now it actually seemed a little shy. "Do you know any stories?"

Stories? What did that have to do with anything? But it was probably best to answer, even though the question seemed so senseless. "Yeah, sure I do," I said.

"And how about your friend? Does she know stories, too?"

I looked over at Katie. She was struggling to escape, red-faced, gasping for breath. I was struggling almost as hard as she was—even though I knew that being eaten was inevitable.

"Sure," I told the crab, gasping, too. "She reads as much as I do. But why do you care whether we know—"

I was interrupted by orders in their own language from the other crab. The part of me that was glad to be here looked around for the first time since we had been captured.

We had entered a very large clearing in the jungle. Above the middle of the clearing reared a gigantic balloon, painted with intricate designs of many bright colors, like a gorgeous Oriental carpet. The woven basket underneath the balloon was big enough to hold many individuals. It was tethered to the ground by thick ropes, creaking with the strain of holding it down.

The crabs were speaking and rushing around, very well organized, shooting behind them with wooden things like crossbows—crossbows that could cause explosions. The other aliens must be after us again.

The crabs scurried sideways fast through an opening in the basket and quickly tied Katie and me to shackles made of fibers. But they didn't hurt or pinch; they were, in fact, very luxurious, since they were attached to spongy reclining chairs clearly designed for humanoids, more comfortable than anything on the ships on which we had spent so much time. There were even window openings in the basket at exactly the right height and location so that from our seated positions we could see outside, without having to stand up and look over the edge of the basket. Most of the crabs scrambled inside with us, but two stayed outside to untie the ropes and fend off the others.

Katie was fighting against the shackles. I remembered what they were going to do to us and started wrestling against the ropes, too.

"Sorry we have to tie you down," one of the crabs explained to us. "We would prefer to let you freely enjoy this experience. But in olden days, when our ancestors allowed freedom to other guests of your species, they jumped out, preferring to die as soon as possible, because of the very unfair reputation we seem to have among so many species. Of course they weren't fit to eat after dying that way. But you can still enjoy the view from where you sit."

Katie had stopped struggling for a moment. We looked at each other, baffled. "This wasn't what the rule book said they were like," I whispered to her.

"I just want *out!*" she muttered, and started tugging at the ropes again.

The balloon shot up with a tremendous surge. The basket rocked when something hit it—a weapon from one of the others—but it kept right on going. When the jungle trees were far below us, its rate of ascension slowed.

"But those other creatures want me for their game," I told the crab. "They need me. Can't they shoot this thing down? Wouldn't it be safer for you to travel by land or in a real plane?"

The crab didn't seem the least bit fazed by the others. "Momentarily we will be out of range of their weapons. Look outside! Enjoy!" it cried excitedly. "Enjoy the lovely view!"

It was odd to hear such ecstatic jubilance over beauty coming from such a viciously monstrous-looking thing. Katie was too upset to pay attention. I looked out the windows—while at the same time I kept thrashing against the ropes. To struggle was as automatic as sneezing.

The view was indeed spectacular. As the land sloped

upward, the jungle trees diminished, and we passed over rolling grasslands, dotted with pinks and purples and yellows that must have been patches of wildflowers. A wide river splashed through it, sparkling in the sunlight; the water was so clear that even from this height I could see the white sandy bottom. The hills grew steeper and more rocky, with neat winding paths snaking up them, and long thin waterfalls, and occasional small stone buildings with colored flags fluttering, perhaps some kind of temples or shrines.

Now the shining snowcapped mountains appeared in the distance. But before we got very close to the mountains, the city came into view. It was surrounded by stone ramparts, but because there were no holes in the ramparts for shooting through, and because there were no guns, and because the ramparts were smooth and winding and planted with flowering shrubs, it was clear they were intended not as protection from invaders but as promenades from which to enjoy the scenery. We were getting lower now, clearly heading for the city. I could see pairs of crabs strolling claw in claw along the promenade, stopping to watch us when they noticed we were coming, and other crabs sitting at low tables, having picnics.

Inside the walls the city was all hills, with many steep streets. None of the redbrick buildings were very high, the tallest only a few stories, most with wooden roofs, some with many layers of decorative roofs, like pagodas. There were parks with waterfalls and streaming banners, and sculptured fountains, and large paved squares with statues where little crabs scampered and bigger ones sat dining on flat round stones laden with abundant food.

Beautifully designed curving stairways, shaded by trees, connected the many different levels of the city, and there were also winding ramps for the wooden vehicles. It would be a great pleasure to live in this high city.

Katie didn't seem to be noticing any of it. She had given up struggling but was just sitting there gasping, her eyes down. And that made me remember that they were going to break our legs and leave us lying there, and then occasionally amputate our limbs and eat them. I groaned and tugged hard at my own ropes again.

The large grassy landing ground had storage sheds around the edges, probably for other balloons. We gradually descended and touched the earth gently.

I turned to Katie. "Oh, if only they weren't going to eat us!" I said, even though at the same time I was expecting it to happen.

"No!" Katie said, like a sob, and shrank back against the basket wall. My eyes filled with tears and I shrank back, too.

And now there was bustle as they unlocked us from our shackles and gently picked me up again. Writhing and panting, we were carried to a wooden cart with four large wheels and a beautifully draped golden canopy on top, with red fringes. The seats were comfortably upholstered in red plush. We were attached firmly in place again with ropes around our feet and legs. Our hands were left free. The driver perched on a delicately carved wooden seat in the front, and he actually managed to make a gesture like a bow to us, despite his crab anatomy. He flicked the reins.

The two animals pulling the cart were something like

goats, goats with big blue eyes and delicately curved horns. Their white-and-black-patterned fur was long and curly and spotlessly clean, and their hooves clicked pleasantly on the paving stones when we left the grassy field of the landing ground.

The crabs we passed bowed to us, too: the crabs dining in the city's outdoor cafés, even those waiting in line to buy delicacies from outdoor stalls.

They sure liked to eat a lot. They were also very polite.

And finally Katie began to notice what was happening around us. She shook her head in wonderment and misery. "You know, we're being taken to the guillotine in a tumbrel, like in *A Tale of Two Cities*. But they act more like we're Queen Elizabeth."

"Yeah. It's like a dream," I said. "Especially after being on that yucky ship for a week."

"No dream. A *nightmare!*" she snarled, and began pulling at the ropes on her feet again. So I did, too.

And my feet came loose. I looked down at them, confused.

Katie had seen the ropes around my feet come undone. "Run, Barney!" she whispered urgently. "Now's your chance!"

I leaned over, first making sure the driver wasn't looking, and tied the ropes again. "What's the point?" I said to Katie. "How could we escape from here anyway, walled in, with crabs everywhere?"

"You could *try!*" she begged me. "You could jump out and run and try to get back to the others, and then they'd help you come back and get me. Go on! Untie the rope again and jump out now!"

I sighed. "It wouldn't work."

She shook her head at me in miserable bewilderment. "Barney, what's the *matter* with you? I'd run the second I had the chance!"

"Look around at this incredible city," I told her, without any hope that she would pay attention. She glared down at her feet. I turned away from her and stared outside the carriage. I was bewildered by my own behavior, too, and wished she hadn't seen.

The city was no less beautiful from the ground than it had been from the air. The ancient redbrick buildings were artfully designed and constructed, with curving stonework holding up intricately carved wooden window frames and balconies, some painted dusty rose, some natural wood, from which crabs, having a peaceful meal in the afternoon sun, bowed down at us. Some of the buildings had multitiered roofs, held up by carved wooden columns. Fountains of dragons and lions and other storybook beasts plashed as we passed a green park. The trees rustled above us, making flickering shadows. Up a curving ramp in the bright cool air—the landing field had not been in the highest part of the city. There were spaces between the buildings here, from which I could see down through the curving streets to many other beautiful houses, and what might be temples with big white domes, mysterious eyes painted on the surface. I could even get glimpses over the rampart walls to the shining snowy mountains on one side and the foothills on the other.

Okay, I was scared, too, of myself as well as the crabs, and Katie was making me feel like a coward. But I had never been anyplace so beautiful—or so peaceful and civilized—in my life.

13

As we ascended I began to notice that the houses and other buildings were getting fancier. Some buildings had crabs standing at attention in front of them, like guards, who checked other crabs before letting them go inside. We seemed to be reaching the highest—and most important—neighborhood in the city.

Katie was still staring sullenly down at her shoes. It was *Katie* who was behaving normally and naturally, as one *should* behave in this situation. So what was the matter with me that I wasn't as scared—and as determined to escape—as she was?

But there it was. I was almost enjoying myself here. And since escape was certainly impossible, despite what Katie said, it was probably just as well that I wasn't in a torment of misery like she was.

And finally the carriage slowed as it approached what was clearly a very important building. It was the first building I had seen that was entirely carved out of dark wood. It was in good repair, but also seemed more ancient in design than any of the other buildings. There was so much carving on it—more primitive than on the other buildings—and so many balconies that there were no flat planks at all in its construction. Crabs in the carvings intertwined in various strange positions, and humanoids, too. In a lot of the carvings the crabs were doing things to people, but it was hard to tell exactly what. It was black inside the windows. I felt scared again. This building might be important, but it was also ominous—it cast an aura of gloom in the bright sunlight.

What looked at first like a tall, decorative metal fence surrounded it. As we stopped in front of the gate I could see that the fence was not merely decorative for the sake of being grand. The poles of the fence were too close together for a person to squeeze through, and the ornamentations at the top were like razor-sharp arrows. Once you went in here, you couldn't get out, unless they let you out.

And what reason did they have to let us out?

The very elaborate golden gate slid open. The carriage started toward it.

Katie was staring hard and pleadingly at me. And suddenly my calmness dissolved. This was it! The building looked magnificent in an eerie way, but what it really was was a prison and slaughterhouse—for us.

This was my last chance. Katie was tied up, but I could

get my feet loose in a second. I slid over to jump out of the carriage before it went through the gate.

And the instant before I jumped, a feeling of vast relief flowed through me. This building wasn't eerie, it was welcoming—and it was exactly where I wanted to be, more than anywhere else.

"Go ahead, Barney! Jump! *Now!*" Katie urged me, lurching against the ropes.

I was poised. But the relief at being here was so strong that all I did was relax back onto the comfortable cushions. Escape was impossible. Who needed to be chased and caught?

As the carriage entered the enclosure, Katie was still staring at me. But her expression had changed. She looked afraid of me, her eyes sliding. "Barney," she whispered. "Why . . . why didn't you run?"

I shook my head. "I don't know," I said. "I was going to, but something stopped me. Something made me *want* to go in here."

We stared at each other. Was I as pale as Katie? The gate clanged shut with finality behind us.

Two crabs in gloves removed each of us from the carriage. Now we both struggled harder than ever. Somehow I knew that this was the most important moment to be terrified.

Another crab bustled sideways over to us, recognizably different from the others. It was larger, for one thing. The heaviness in the underbelly indicated that it was not genetically bigger, just fatter. There were pretty touches of orange in its green carapace. And its mouth was larger, and more mobile. It actually seemed to be smiling at us.

It turned to face us. And this crab really *was* able to bow, bending over so much that its fat belly actually scraped against the paving stones. "Welcome, welcome, my dear honored guests!" it cried, in the best English a crab had spoken yet. "Allow me to introduce myself, please. My name is Abamee. From now on I will be your chief host, your servant, your chef—and in the end, your liberator."

Then it waddled carefully around us, examining us closely. I whimpered and thrashed. It said something to the other crabs in their own language, the crabs that were having such a hard time keeping a grip on us. They answered. The crab that called itself Abamee seemed pleased with the answer—pleased that we were so desperate to get away?

"May I urge you to try to relax?" Abamee said. "You have passed the test; you are healthy and clean of infection. And no matter how hard you try, there is no way you can escape. Soon we will give you something to help you relax, but for your own sake, try to be a little calmer now. Please? Can you tell me your names?"

"I'm, er, Barney," I said, sweat breaking out on my body as I felt the most peculiar mixture yet of horror and serenity. I gulped. "And this is Katie," I said, nodding in her direction as she writhed in the claws of the two crabs who were holding her.

Abamee said pleasantly, "Welcome, Barney. Welcome, Katie," just as though we were not being held there by force. It paused, and then asked almost tentatively, "Is it possible that you might . . ." Abamee looked down sheepishly for a moment—and looking sheepish couldn't be easy for a crab. "Is it possible that . . . you might know any stories?"

Stories? There it was again. What was this thing they had about stories?

"Well, yeah, I guess I do," I said. Why not try to please it? "And Katie does, too."

Abamee bounced around and clicked both its claws separately above its head, sort of like a fat Spanish dancer with gigantic castanets. "Oh, we have jolly times in store for us indeed!" it cried. "Welcome, welcome again! We usually start with a tour of your residence and the facilities, which often helps to make humans feel a bit more comfortable about being here. Come, come, let us begin." It bowed again, and gestured toward the doors of the dark looming building.

Abamee led the way. The crabs carried us behind it.

And after they had brought us through the heavily carved doorway into the cool darkness inside, Abamee hurried behind and locked the door with several different keys. It said something to the crabs and they gently put us down. But they still hovered near us.

Even though I knew it was useless, I followed Katie's example and ran back to the door and banged and pulled at the handle, until she fell back, exhausted from her struggles.

"No, no, you're going to have to give all that up, I'm afraid," Abamee told us. "There is no way out. Please, just accept—and try to enjoy."

"Enjoy?" Katie said, gasping. It was the first word she had spoken to a crab. "What's to enjoy? You're going to torture and kill us."

Abamee put one claw to the side of his face, somehow managing to look worried and concerned for us. "Oh, dear me," it said. "Why do so many humanoid species get these terrible ideas about us? It must be that they only know about our history. We are far more civilized now. You are about to begin a process that will probably be the most pleasurable experience of your young lives."

"Being eaten by you?" Katie said. "You *are* going to eat us, right?"

"All in good time, all in good time," Abamee said, not denying it. It gestured at one of the waiting crabs, and it scurried off. "But what you don't understand is the process of preparation—very careful preparation. Come, let us retire to the first atrium while our friend brings you something that will help you to relax. Please, admire the glorious ancient architecture of your palace." And it gestured with its claw like a tour guide.

It was dark in here, and not easy to see the intricate carvings and the murals on the walls after being in the bright sunlight. But ahead of us was an arched opening flooded with light. Abamee waddled toward it. The guards behind us moved forward. We had no choice but to follow.

We stepped out into a courtyard, surrounded on four sides by the wooden building, a large balcony going all the way around the second floor. Suddenly it was warm again in the sunlight. Brick pathways wound through the garden of bright pink, yellow, and red blossoms. In the center of the courtyard a rectangular pool sparkled, paved with pale green stone, the water crystal clear. Benches surrounded the pool, designed for humans, not crabs. The guards prodded us gently until we sat down by the water.

It occurred to me that this place was open to the sky—we could be beamed up from here. In a moment I forgot that idea.

Abamee stood before us and gestured upward, its eyes quivering on their slender stalks. "Please, look carefully. This entire residence is a marvelous work of art. It is my great privilege to be its guardian—and your privilege to enjoy every aspect of its brilliant concept and design."

Katie slumped over hopelessly and didn't even bother to look up. I studied the heavily carved balcony, its railing, its curved supports, the dark windows and occasional doors behind it.

And then I detected movement behind one of the second-floor windows, and shadowy shapes—not crab shapes, humanoid shapes. In a moment they were gone.

"Yes, yes, we have it now, look here, look here, now you will feel better," Abamee said quickly, suddenly *not* wanting me to look up at the balcony. The crab he had ordered away had come back with a woven tray, and on it were two gleaming blue ceramic cups. "Drink now. Drink, and all will be well."

Katie stiffened and pressed her lips together as the tray was offered to us. Maybe this was it—the poison that would kill us.

"Please be aware that we cannot eat poisoned flesh," Abamee said. "Nor can we eat flesh that has not been carefully prepared, and that takes a period of time. This soothing drink will only make you feel better." It paused, and its voice became just a bit less kind. "And in any case, you have no choice. Drink."

Somehow I knew this was not poison, and that it was to my advantage to drink it. I lifted one of the cups.

Katie moved to knock it out of my hand. But the guard behind her moved faster, gripping her arms with its gloved claws.

"Drink," Abamee said again. I drank.

Whatever it was worked fast. I began to feel warm and deeply relaxed. Tension drained out of every muscle. The flowers were brighter, the pool more inviting. I wanted to shed my clothes and fall in. Even Abamee didn't look so hideous. He was beaming encouragingly at me, so happy that I felt so good. I couldn't help grinning back at him.

I turned to Katie, feeling radiant. "Drink it, Katie! It's fantastic!" I urged her.

"You believe them? You believe they're not just poisoning us?" she said grimly.

"If all they were going to do was poison us, why would they bring us to live here?" I asked her, understanding everything better now. "Why would they talk about the period of preparation? If this is what it feels like . . . *Wow!*"

"Drink, my dear, for your own good," Abamee said kindly. And Abamee *was* kind, I sensed it very strongly now.

Katie sat there with her fists clenched, staring straight ahead of her.

"Believe me, we know what we are doing—the procedure has been refined over centuries," Abamee told her. It clicked a claw at the guards.

The crab holding her arms tightened its grip. Another pulled back her head and held her jaw open. A third poured the drink into her mouth. She tried to resist, she choked, she gagged a little. But some of the drink went down.

And it was enough. I watched her. With my new clarity of vision I could see the struggle going on inside her to fight the effects of the drink, to remain resistant. But it was impossible. She visibly brightened. The guards let go of her and put the cup down. Her hand moved slowly, she was still trying to fight it. But she couldn't. She grabbed the cup and drained it.

And then she turned to me. "So strange," she murmured. "I still hate it here, I'm still terrified, but . . . I can stand it now." But she still didn't smile at me.

"You see?" Abamee said. "Abamee is always right. Trust Abamee. He knows what is best for you. Come, let us take a little walk before I show you to your quarters."

We walked on a flowered path around the pool. "You will bathe here frequently," Abamee told us, "in different marinades, each more refreshing and delicious than the last. And you can relax here in the clear mountain air." He gestured at a row of reclining chairs made out of something like canvas and wood that looked very comfortable indeed.

Into a doorway, down a dark corridor with murals and carvings, out into another courtyard. Though there were flowers here, too, this one looked more functional than the first, with taps and hoses and large ceramic vats of various substances, and padded tables for lying on. "Mud baths here. Very good for the skin," Abamee explained. "And gentle abrasives, too, for toning."

Inside again. Abamee opened a door and was enveloped in aromatic steam. "Steam bath here, as you can see. Sauna over here." Down another corridor. This place was bigger than it had looked from the outside, and labyrinthine. Already I had no idea how to get back to the first atrium, or the entrance. "Massage room," Abamee said as we passed a room with more padded tables and shelves of what were probably various lotions, ointments, and oils in ornamental jars.

Farther along, from another opening that led downstairs came the sound of pots banging and smells so delicious that I could feel myself begin to salivate. "The kitchen. The food is always wonderful, but tonight's dinner will be special, to celebrate your arrival."

As wonderful as it smelled, the thought of the kitchen in this place was scary to me. I hurried past. The effects of the drink, and Abamee's constant chatter, helped to nullify the bad feeling.

We started up a flight of stairs; Abamee climbed sideways, rocking back and forth rather comically as he mounted. "Of course, this is only the beginning; there are more pleasures here. But now I will take you to your quarters, where you can rest comfortably. You were brought here in alien craft, I was told, so I don't imagine the trip was very comfortable for you."

"It sure wasn't," I said, remembering Julian's ship—but also missing him, in an odd way.

"Barney's was worse than mine," Katie added.

Abamee looked back eagerly at us. "Perhaps, over dinner—if you will allow me to join you—you could tell me stories from your trip? Stories of how you came here? I do so love human stories. We all do."

On Julian's ship I had grown used to eating in a disgusting situation, so having Abamee at the table with us would be no problem for me. I glanced at Katie. The drink had altered her mood to the extent that she said, "Sure, we'll tell you. Why not?" But there was still misery in her voice.

We had reached the top of the stairs and were heading down another corridor. And I heard distant voices—not crab voices, weeping human voices.

Instantly Abamee started talking loudly, hurrying us along. "I'm sure you need to rest comfortably after your long, unpleasant trip. Here are your quarters. I hope you will find them acceptable—as I said, we have long experience with people of your species. We will not disturb you. Ring the bell when you are rested and ready to eat—ring it at any time at all, whenever you need anything. Your whims are our commands."

Abamee ushered us through a doorway, then bowed and backed out. The door closed. We could hear it being locked from the outside.

"Our whims may be their commands, but we're still locked up," Katie said, in a dull and hopeless tone of voice I had never heard before we got here.

We looked around. It wasn't just a room, it was a suite. We were in the living room. The furniture did not look exactly like Earth furniture, but it did appear to be comfortable. There were two large couches and a low table between them, and several big easy chairs. All the furniture was deeply padded and there were lots of pillows. What made it not like Earth were the designs woven into the upholstery fabrics. The colors were tastefully muted, yet lively, and the patterns so imaginative and complex that you could be entertained for a long time by just staring at them, following the twists and turns with your eyes.

Against one wall was a bar, loaded with all kinds of drinks and snacks in decanters and baskets.

We walked over to a large window that overlooked the mountains. There was also a door opening out onto a balcony, but there would be no escaping that way. When we stepped out we saw that this side of the building was on the very edge of a deep, deep chasm. Directly underneath the balcony, a sheer rock wall plunged down thousands of feet. It made me a little dizzy, and I gripped the railing to steady myself. Even if someone *wanted* to jump—and they had told us that people had jumped from the balloon in the past—there was a tough-looking screen from balcony ceiling to floor that sealed it off from the chasm. And the balcony did not lead to any other part of the building—it was blocked off at each end by wooden walls. Still, there were comfortable-looking chairs and a table out here so that we could sit and admire the view, and nibble and sip. It was a luxurious prison.

We went back in. On either side of the living room was a bedroom, and each bedroom had its own bath. Again, the bathrooms were not exactly like Earth bathrooms; they were wooden, but each had a tub and a shower and a sink and reasonable toilet—wooden toilets that flushed!—and piles of big thick soft towels, and cabinets of soaps and shampoos and perfumes in beautiful glass jars.

Back in the living room, I said, "He was right about it being comfortable here, too."

Katie nodded. "More luxurious than anyplace *I've* ever lived," she agreed. "I bet if I took a nap I might even be hungry." She banged one hand against her head. "How come I'm not scared anymore?"

"That drink," I reminded her, stuffing some of the pretzel-like snacks into my mouth.

"What are you eating that for?" Katie asked me, sounding worried again. "Who knows what it is? Maybe that drink made me less scared, but I'm still never going to understand why you didn't run when you had the chance."

I wanted to change the subject. "There's the bell to ring when we want to eat, or anything else."

The bell sat on the low wooden table, large and made out of some kind of metal, and looked heavy. Like everything else in this city, it was ornate, complex patterns molded deeply into it. I wondered what all the patterns meant.

"When we were in that first courtyard, I thought I saw some people in one of the windows on the second floor," I told Katie. "And later on I heard human voices, crying. Did you hear them?"

"No." She looked scared again. "Are you sure about that?"

"Pretty sure," I said. "They could be people . . . in an advanced stage of preparation." The idea chilled me, even with the drink and everything else.

Katie shook her head. "I can't deal with anything now. I'm exhausted." She yawned. "I've got to lie down. Don't ring the bell until I come back in here. And don't keep eating those snacks, you jerk."

I was hurt by her coldness. But I said, "I'm wiped out, too. Which bedroom do you want?"

"Doesn't matter—they both look exactly the same. I'll take this one," she said, gesturing to the right.

And then, out of nowhere, a crab appeared in the middle of the room.

We both jumped and I almost screamed. We hadn't seen a real crab appear out of nowhere like this. Yes, Abamee had told us about the long period of preparation. But maybe this was a rogue crab, less refined, that could teleport itself and wanted to eat us *now*, without any preparation at all.

It was not a pleasant-looking crab. It was not smiling, like Abamee. We both ran for the bell.

"G'day, mates," the crab said. "Comfy digs the famous crabs gave you, didn't they."

14

"Julian!"

We weren't dumb enough to shout his name; we whispered. But of course we were both overjoyed that he had come.

"Why do you have to look like *that*?" I asked him.

"Protective coloring."

"Yeah, but if a crab came in, you couldn't talk crab to it, and it would know," Katie pointed out. "Can't you look like something else?"

"Would you like me to appear as I really am?" he asked teasingly.

"Forget it," she said quickly.

I thought of something else. "What if they have a hidden camera in here, or a microphone—bugging devices?"

"This species has not advanced technologically in that direction. Remember the balloon, the crossbows? Why, these blokes are practically medieval!"

"Shhh! Don't talk so loud," Katie said. "Just get us out of here. You could beam us from that courtyard."

Crab Julian laughed. It was not a pretty sight, with all those teeth. "I'm afraid it's not that easy, my dear. First of all, I'm not really here—you know this is just a projection. Of course all of the players want you, Barney, because of your lichen immunity. And Katie, too, as a prod for you. So nobody wants you to be eaten. But they're also so suspicious of each other and terrified that one of the others will get you first, that they will blow up any ship that gets near this place to try to beam you up. They're quite nasty—they have major problems working together, and it's going to take them a while to learn how. So no one can beam you out of here. They only let me come because I can't do anything in this form. You two have gotten yourselves into a fine mess for everyone, believe me."

"*We* got ourselves into this? It was *you* guys who brought us here," Katie hotly pointed out.

"You mean none of the aliens with all their attributes will do *anything*?" I said.

"I didn't say that exactly. But it's going to take some clever planning, and the others aren't easy to deal with. Luckily we have a bit of time. We're working on it. But you two have to help, too. Keep your eyes and ears open for any possible means of escape. Barney, you know what your other alien friends can and can't do. I'll be checking back when it seems safe."

"What about Jrlb, the fish man?" I asked him. "He has access to hyperspace—he can go anywhere on this planet in an instant. Couldn't he get in here and just take us back with him?"

"Believe me, he would if he could, my lad. But that's one of the rules of the hyperspace card. Its user cannot take anyone with him. But it's just as well. If he *could* get you out of here with his card on his own, he'd just make you get The Piggy for him and then kill you. Cheery-bye, then. I'd better get out of here before the crabs notice or hear anything." He waved with a claw and was gone.

Katie and I just looked at each other. There was nothing to say. The drink had cheered us for a while. But it was wearing off now—especially after Julian's assessment of how hopeless our situation was. We just sighed and went to our bedrooms.

It was the most comfortable bed I had ever lain down on. Amazingly, I slept. I hadn't slept well on Julian's ship, and the events since our arrival here had been exhausting. Perhaps the drink had something to do with it, too, because I didn't dream—which was probably just as well.

It was dark when I woke up. A softly glowing lantern had been lit by the side of the bed, and a fresh set of clothes was neatly laid out on a chair.

A crab had been in here while I was sleeping. That was a very creepy feeling.

But I was grateful for the clean clothes. I heard water running from the other room. A real shower with soap would be heavenly.

Katie was waiting in the living room when I came in, all cleaned up. She was wearing a loose-fitting cotton pajama-type outfit, just like mine, though hers was a pale lavender and mine was dark blue. It looked better on her. "One of them was in here while we were asleep," I said.

"Duh?" she said, and wrapped her arms around herself. "I don't know if I'll be able to sleep again, knowing they come in and out like that."

"Tell Abamee. He'll give us something to help us sleep. And they'll probably have more of that drink with dinner."

She looked disappointed in me, but she said, "I'm starving. I can't help it. The food was lousy on Soma's ship."

"Yeah," I said. "The food on Julian's ship was like airplane food—in certain ways they haven't made much progress. But want to take a look at the view for a second first?"

She shrugged and followed me.

We stepped out onto the balcony. And the first thing we noticed was not the view, or the stars.

It was a human voice, screaming in pain.

And in the sky over the mountains there were fireworks, spectacular fireworks, more elaborate than anything on Earth. Fireworks that seemed to be telling stories, different shapes appearing and fading as they fell. Some kind of gala celebration was going on.

And a human was screaming.

This time Katie heard it, too. She looked at me with her hand over her mouth. Because this wall of the building was on the edge of a cliff, and because the balcony was blocked off at both ends, we could see nothing of the rest of the building from here. But the scream seemed to be coming from inside.

And then the scream was abruptly cut off. Fireworks splashed across the mountainsides and the snowy peaks in dazzling reds and greens, silver and gold.

"Do you think they're going to feast tonight?" I said. "Is that what the celebration is about?"

We went quickly back into the living room. "I'm not so hungry anymore," Katie said.

"Me either. But we've got to eat."

"But . . . what's going on? And can we trust what they give us from that kitchen?"

Of course I knew what she was saying: What if they fed us the flesh of their other victims?

"I don't think they'd do that," I said. "It's their favorite food. It doesn't make sense for them to feed us something they love and we can't stand."

"But—does it come from the same kitchen? The same pots and pans?"

"I've heard that human flesh is supposed to taste like pork," I said. "Just—avoid anything that looks or smells like pork. Everything about this place is so luxurious. The food probably will be, too. Let's just do it." And before she could stop me, I picked up the bell and shook it.

It made a surprisingly deep sound, that seemed oddly to come from a long way away. It rang in our ears for almost a minute after I put it down.

We waited restlessly. In a very short time there was a

knock at the door. "May I come in?" Abamee's voice asked from the corridor.

"Why not? Somebody was already in here while we were asleep," Katie called back.

Locks clicked, the door opened, and Abamee beckoned to us. "Only a servant, to bring you fresh clothes. We know humans like to bathe and change their clothing frequently. She wouldn't harm you, believe me. And your dirty clothes will be taken away and cleaned and returned to you. Come. Dine with me."

He led us downstairs and around several corridors to a wood-paneled room with a rectangular table and a fire burning cheerfully in a brick hearth. There were two chairs and two place settings, and a funny cushionlike thing across from them. Abamee did not sit down upon it until after we had taken our seats. There was a basket of what looked very much like bread, a shallow bowl of oil, and on each plate were slices of something like smoked salmon and a piece of cheese. A goblet of pale amber liquid sat beside each plate.

"Let me assure you before we say anything else that we certainly do *not* feed our guests the flesh of their own species. That would be rude and distasteful," Abamee said, turning down his mouth in disapproval. "Not to mention, it is a precious commodity and it would be wasteful in the extreme to give it to anyone who does not appreciate it. Drink, and then try your appetizers. And if there is anything that is not one hundred percent to your satisfaction, please tell me immediately and it will be replaced."

The drink was similar to the other one in that it relaxed us and enhanced our senses. The flames became brighter and more cheerful, the room cozier. The difference was that *this* drink also made us ravenous. Everything—the bread, the olive oil, the fish, the cheese—was utterly delicious. Even with all her cookbooks and her fancy equipment, Mom had never come close to anything like this. We gobbled it down as Abamee watched with a benign expression. He did not even try to ask us to tell any stories yet. He knew we were too busy eating to be able to talk.

When we finished he rang a little bell, and immediately another crab entered, took our used plates away, put more food in front of us, and refilled our glasses from an ancient-looking bottle. It was amazing how clever they were with their claws. But then the claws were quite sharp and delicate at the ends, and they were opposable, so it was as though they had a thumb.

This food was clearly recognizable as fowl of some kind—each plate had a drumstick and a breast, juicy and succulent, with a beautiful creamy sauce on it and a sprinkling of fresh herbs. There was also something that looked like crisply fried potatoes, a green vegetable of some kind, and a salad in a separate bowl. "Please, eat your fill. There are second helpings, of course. We urge you to eat as much as possible. No reason for you two string beans to worry about gaining weight! And remember that there will be dessert."

We dug in. Now that the edge had been taken off our hunger, we were able to take the time to say, "Wonderful!" "Delicious!" "I've never had anything this good in my *life!*"

Abamee beamed happily at us. "The story of your trip?" he gently prompted us.

But before we had a chance to tell him very much at all, another crab hurried in. It said something to Abamee in an undertone, and suddenly his expression changed. "Excuse me, my friends. I must leave you for a moment. Enjoy!" He was trying to sound cheerful, but there was an edge of worry in his voice that I had never heard before. He and the other crab rushed out of the room.

This was the first time we had been left alone and not locked up since our arrival here. We looked at each other and didn't even have to speak: This might be our only chance to see *something* of what was really going on in this place. We left the wonderful food and hurried quietly out into the corridor.

Abamee and the other crab were going as fast as they could, but their anatomy made it easy for us to keep up with them. It also made it risky for us to follow. With their flexible eyes and sideways stance, the crabs could see backward as well as forward, but seemed too intent now on their destination to glance back at us. We saw each turn they made. In my head I repeated the directions—*left, left, right, left*—so that we'd be able to get back to the dining room on our own.

We followed Abamee and the other crab down a flight of stairs. It was noticeably warmer here, and there was a burning smell. Down here there were no carvings and no murals. The walls were rough stone, not wood. The two crabs entered a room with an open metal doorway. We looked at each other, then crept up to the door and peeked in around the edge.

The room was very hot. The walls were covered with a strange, mottled material that looked like soundproofing.

And inside the room was the biggest fireplace I had ever seen, at least ten feet by ten feet. Inside the fireplace stood a grill for cooking meat—big enough to broil a couple of cows at one time. But it was not cows that were gagged and strapped down to two tables like stretchers on wheels.

One of the young women was blond, the other brunette. They looked like they could have been attractive once—before they had gotten so fat. They struggled and thrashed on the tables. The crabs on duty tonight did not seem to be used to dealing with people struggling like this before being roasted.

Roasted alive, it was clear, because they were not doing anything to make them unconscious. Perhaps they were more delicious that way, without any drugs in their bodies. Obviously, we had rung for Abamee at an inconvenient time. Perhaps the rest of the crabs here were young and inexperienced.

"Oh, Nicole. Oh, Abbie," Abamee said to the young women. "Please behave! This is your moment of glory, the end result of all your lovely preparation."

And then Abamee immediately began barking orders to the younger crabs. Quickly, one of the women was wrapped in ropes that were not attached to the stretcher on which she lay. Her straps were removed and she was lifted, struggling more wildly than ever.

And I saw then the metal manacles attached to the broiling-hot grate. The crabs carried her toward the manacles above the smoking fire. We could see its bright glow reflected on the walls and on her rosy bulging flesh as they approached.

Katie was now gesturing frantically. She wanted to go,

she couldn't bear to watch for another instant, and she was also afraid of being caught. She was right on all counts.

And still I felt reluctant to leave this hot torture chamber. I wanted to watch for just another minute . . .

Katie gestured again, angrily. I knew she was right. A crab might come to the dining room and find us missing. Reluctantly I dragged myself away from the metal door and led the way back. The dining room was still empty. We sat down.

"You can eat now?" Katie asked me.

"We have to, or he'll know. Have more to drink. That'll help."

"The people . . . they have to be conscious," Katie said faintly. "They're not even humane enough to knock them out. It must be so *slow*. Worse than Joan of Arc being burned at the stake—that went fast. I . . . I don't . . ."

I was scared, too. But what scared me more than what we had just seen was that I was not as sickened as Katie was. What was the matter with me? I couldn't stand to think about it. *"Drink!"* I ordered her, and took a big gulp myself. I felt better immediately. "Look, we'll get out of here somehow. All those other aliens want us. We're keeping our eyes open, like Julian said. But if Abamee finds out what we just saw, we'll have even *less* chance of getting away. You can do it if you just drink some more of this stuff. We can't let them know what we saw."

Katie drank. But she didn't gulp it down like I did, she only took one sip. She was smarter than me; she wanted to be clearheaded. Still, it calmed her down. We ate.

Abamee came back, looking flustered. "Just a minor

problem," he said. "But stress always makes me raven-ous." He was staring at us in a strange way, his lipless mouth slightly parted. "I'd . . . I'd better order some food, quickly." He rang the bell.

And we were somehow able to act normally and tell him our stories. He loved them, more relaxed now after eating. "You're both *marvelous!*" he told us, over the chocolate torte with caramel custard sauce. "I haven't run across such good storytellers in years! Yes, this *will* be the jolliest of times."

And so our stay in this palace of pleasure began, just as the stay of the two young women before us was slowly ending.

15

Madame Gondii was getting very impatient.

She had been thrilled when Barney had gotten so close to the fire where they were about to cook the other humans. She had rushed to her own kitchen, of course. She wanted to delay Barney, make him curious and careless, so that the crabs would see him spying, and catch him and cook and eat him then and there.

But she hadn't been prepared for it. She had been relaxing once it was clear that Barney could never escape from this place. And before she could mix the right hormones and make them strong enough to keep him there, his human companion had gotten him away from the crab kitchen. Madame Gondii cursed the girl and cursed herself for letting that happen.

The crabs had to eat him soon. Her time was running out.

But the crabs did *not* eat him soon. The next day, after a rich breakfast, he soaked in the pool of lightly seasoned liquid with his friend. The pool was not big enough to actually swim in—the crabs did not want them to get much exercise, it seemed. A large lunch was followed by another crab pummeling his body, which seemed to make him feel good, and then smearing some kind of glop on him and letting it sit there for a while, before washing him off carefully. He was given a midafternoon snack, then sat in a very hot room, full of steam—but not hot enough to cook him, unfortunately. Another stint in the pool in a slightly stronger liquid followed. After that, he relaxed in bed, reading one of the books in his own language that the crabs had provided for his entertainment.

They ate another lovely dinner while conversing with the crab who seemed to be in charge.

The next day followed a similar pattern, and the next. And now Madame Gondii began to despair. How long was this going to go on? It might take more time than she had. She hadn't realized that the crabs moved so slowly, that they did not eat human flesh until it had been carefully seasoned and prepared over such a long period of time.

Clearly the crabs had evolved—their treatment of human flesh had changed since she had been taught about them. They seemed to have become more discriminating in their tastes.

But there was an even more chilling possibility. Her little thing like a heart pumped wildly when the thought of it came to her.

Yes, Madame Gondii had made Barney struggle against them so that they would not suspect she was there inside him. But perhaps the crabs had learned that just watching a human struggle was not enough protection against Madame Toxoplasma Gondii and her kind. Perhaps some humans had struggled and been eaten, and yet other Madame Gondiis had still infested the crabs who ate them. The long preparation time might also be a waiting period to give any parasitic organism living within the humans time to die. Then crabs who ate the humans would be safe.

Had they figured out her tricks? Were they even smarter than her species had realized? If so, she was doomed.

She paced in her little cyst, thinking hard and desperately, while Barney was soaked and pummeled and fed. So the crabs had evolved. They had altered their life cycle in order to protect themselves.

Well, perhaps Madame Gondii could evolve as well. After all, she was an expert at mixing hormones—hormones which she most often used on her hosts. But what about herself? There might be hormones she could mix that would prolong her own life cycle. And then one of those beastly crabs—who thought they were so smart—would end up eating her after all. And how she would relish turning it into a sexless zombie whose only function would be to produce thousands more Madame Toxoplasma Gondiis!

She set to work at once. She had the time now. She didn't need to worry about feeding Barney as many hormones anymore. Mainly she just had to keep him hungry, since the fatter he got, the sooner they would eat him. It was also true that if he acted more scared, the crabs would be less suspicious of him. It wouldn't even matter if he and his friend tried to escape.

Because Madame Gondii knew there was no way he was ever going to get out of here.

"Have you taken a look at yourself in the mirror lately, Barney?" Katie asked me, after we had been with the crabs for a while. It was hard to know exactly how long we had been there, the days were so alike, and usually so agreeable—except when I worried, which I was doing more and more often now.

But I still wasn't worrying as much as Katie.

"Mirror?" I said stupidly. And it occurred to me for the first time that the only mirror in our suite of rooms was a very small one over the bathroom sink, just big enough for me to comb my hair and shave, when I needed to. "Yeah, I look in it sometimes. What about it?"

"Have you noticed how round your cheeks are getting? And that *gut*?"

"Gut?" I said, feeling insulted—she said the word with

such disgust. I had never worried about gaining weight. My metabolism worked off whatever I ate, and I'd always been slim and toned. "A gut?" I said again, reaching for my stomach. I felt a scary twinge when I touched it. It had never been this big and soft. Even if I could have seen it in the little mirror, I didn't want to.

Anyway, we weren't in our rooms, we were having our "marination therapy," as Abamee called it, in the strongest—and most aromatic and refreshing—liquid yet. The pool was surrounded by beautiful pale green tiles, and flowering plants, and on a little table lay a pile of big fluffy white towels. Next to the towels were the pitchers of ice water—they were always urging us to drink water.

I took a good look at Katie in her swimsuit. The liquid we were soaking in wasn't clear, it was brownish, as though it had something like soy sauce in it (and it was obvious from the smell that there was something a lot like garlic in it, too). But the marinade was still clear enough for me to see that she was just as slim as ever. "You haven't gained any weight at all," I said. "How come me and not you?"

She sighed. "Because I have half a brain, Barney," she said. "You saw how fat those girls they killed were. They *want* us to be fat. And until we are, they won't eat us. Did you ever hear the story of Hansel and Gretel?" she asked me sarcastically.

I gulped. She was right, of course. Obviously she had been watching what she was eating, to stay too thin for the crabs, to give us—and the aliens who wanted us to survive—more time to figure out an escape plan. Why had I been so stupid?

But I felt more clearheaded now, for some reason—and more afraid. In a way it was kind of a *relief* to be afraid, in contrast to how strangely bland I had felt about the whole situation at first. And now I was getting plumper and more delicious. And there was no reason why they couldn't roast and eat me first, if I was ready before Katie was.

She splashed her fist in the marinade angrily. "What are your friends waiting for? We've spied as much as we could. We can't get out of here without their help. So where are all their super attribute cards you're always talking about?"

She was complaining about the aliens but I knew she was really angry at me. It was time to talk about what was scaring me most.

"Katie—you noticed it, too—something's wrong with me. Wrong about my emotions. It's so *weird* that I haven't been as scared and horrified as you. From the beginning."

She nodded. "You fought at first. But I could feel—I don't know, I could sort of *feel* it was an act. And then you just took to everything so easily." She sounded worried now, too, about me. But even so she was still cold, as though the problem were my fault.

Maybe she *did* care about me after all. I had assumed she didn't. Here we were in this awful situation in which we both needed comfort. Here we were living together in the same suite of rooms, with no parents or anyone else around to prevent us from doing anything we wanted. And yet I hadn't even made a move to touch her. I hadn't, because the feeling of coolness and distance that she projected was palpable. She didn't want us to get physically close. And whatever was making me blasé about the crabs was making me too complacent to try.

I sat up abruptly, the liquid sloshing. "You're right, this has gone on way too long. Julian and Soma and the others aren't doing anything. And the way we're locked up here is pretty hopeless. But we can't just *accept* it." I lowered my voice. "Do you think they're drugging us or something?"

"What do you think that wine stuff is that Abamee is always pouring down our throats? You drink it like there's no tomorrow. I'm sure what it's for is to keep us placid and under control. That's why I drink as little as possible—even though it *does* feel so good." Now she sounded like she might be going to cry. "Oh, Barney, what are we going to do? I have nightmares about those girls who were here before us. I'm going to go *crazy* if we don't get out of here as soon as possible!"

"But what should we do?" I said hopelessly. "Tie our sheets together and climb down a thousand-foot cliff?"

She shook her head. "I don't know. But we've got to think of *something*. And if I were you, I'd go on a diet. The fatter you get, the sooner they'll eat you. And I couldn't stand it, Barney. Being alone here, and . . . and even worse, knowing that terrible thing had happened to you."

We heard a pattering of footclaws as Abamee came scurrying sideways over the pale green glazed tiles to the pool. We were rarely left alone long enough during the day to say even this much to each other, and normally we both fell asleep right after dinner—probably something in the food, and probably another reason we had never gotten any closer.

"Ah, yes, this particular marinade, such a delightful aroma. I hope the two of you are enjoying it." Abamee beamed at me, but then his expression changed when he turned to Katie. "Still so unattractively scrawny, my dear," he said, with a sound like a clucking of teeth. "So unhealthy for you. Clearly the food isn't pleasing you. Can't you tell me what's wrong so I can tell the chefs how to make it more to your liking? We don't *want* you to be undernourished, we want you to enjoy your food, and we work hard at it—we're not like those people in that terrible book by a famous writer from your planet, a story one of our previous guests told me, about a school where the nasty people in charge underfed the students and then punished them if they dared to ask for more."

"*Oliver Twist,* by Dickens," Katie said, and I could tell it was a struggle for her not to add that she would have way preferred to be in that situation than this one. Any sane person would have. But for some reason, even Katie wasn't rude to Abamee. He was always so pleasant and bustling, and his act of caring for our well-being was so total, that it was hard to be nasty to him—even though we knew that his real goal in life was to prepare us for being roasted alive.

He clicked his claws. "Anyway, time for lunch. An unusually good one today, I must say. Perhaps we can even coerce you into having a second helping, Katie, my dear."

I myself was ravenous, as usual, even though we were fed a lot and had no physical activity at all except for walking up a short flight of stairs a couple of times a day. Still, I swore to myself that from now on I would eat less, and maybe even secretly start exercising in the room— do push-ups and sit-ups.

I was struggling to do my tenth sit-up when Julian appeared in crab form. "We've put on a little weight, haven't we," were the first words out of his mouth.

"I'm going to lose it fast," I said defensively.

Earlier, at lunch, Katie had eaten very little of her double-decker ham-and-cheese sandwich, grilled in butter, and none of her deep-fried potatoes, and I had only had one helping, which was unusual for me. It was a struggle, but I managed to resist. We both skipped dessert, even though it was cream puffs with ice cream and whipped cream and chocolate sauce, one of my favorites. Abamee had *not* been pleased. But we knew him now, we knew he would not do anything but act hurt, and I had made the decision earlier that day that hurting Abamee's feelings was something I could deal with.

But I was starving for dinner now. How was I going to deal with that?

I hurried Julian into the living room and got Katie.

"So?" she said. "Any news?"

"We have a plan. Sort of." Julian sounded a bit nervous about it. "It's a compromise born of violence, since no one will let anyone else's ship get near here. So you will have to be rescued by land. They are forced to work together."

"Yeah?" we both said in unison.

"Your friends Zulma and Moyna have finally agreed to

126

go along with it and use their translator disguise selectors. We're pretty sure they'll have a slight accent, but they can pose as visiting dignitaries from another part of the planet, so an accent won't *necessarily* give them away. And they can borrow two more disguise selectors from the others, which they can lend you." He paused, and bit his lipless crab mouth nervously. "They will enter the city as crabs and ask to observe this facility. It's famous all over this world, so that shouldn't seem odd." He stopped, as though unsure about what to say next.

"Yeah? Then what?" Katie said.

"The tricky part is going to be getting you out of here. The guards will naturally wonder where the two extra crabs came from on the way out. The only hope is to drug your guardian, and the guards at the gate to this place. Soma and Jrlb will be waiting on the other side. And since I can't come down to the surface, I have agreed not to beam you up myself—they have promised dire consequences for me if I do. Once you get outside this city, then there'll be a mad race to get you. Quite exciting. Except . . ."

"Except what?" Katie wanted to know.

"Well, we don't have a clue how familiar the crabs are with other species, other than humanoids, of course. We don't know if they know about disguise selectors. We're hoping they *don't* know. That's the gamble. Not everyone is happy with the plan. You two up for it?"

Neither of us said anything for a minute, letting it all sink in. And once it did sink in, my immediate response was, "Isn't that pretty risky? *Too* risky? So many obstacles. And even if we do make it out of the city, then they'll all be fighting for us. You know how hideously vicious they—"

"Shut up, Barney," Katie said. "Let's go for it," she said to Julian. "Getting out of here is worth any risk we have to take."

"But—" I started to say.

"Don't, Barney," she said dangerously. "Even if we *do* get caught, do you think we'll be any worse off than we are now?"

"Yes," I said, and now I didn't feel that it was some weird part of my brain that was talking through me; I felt perfectly logical. "Once we try to escape, and fail, they'll guard us twice as heavily as they do already. And then we'll really never get out of here. We have one chance to try for an escape. This one doesn't seem good enough to me."

"I have to say, I can't completely disagree with you, mate," Julian said, and his crab projection shrugged. "Only, we can't come up with anything else. It's this or nothing, unless you could learn how to fly."

"Julian," I said. "I know that what you care about the most is getting The Piggy. But somehow I thought—on the trip to this planet and all—that you started to like me a little, that we might even kind of be friends. And if we're friends, then—" I felt something like a hand cutting off my breath, so that I literally couldn't speak.

They were both staring at me. It was hard to read the crab Julian's expression, but Katie looked definitely worried. "Barney, what's happening to you? Why did you start to say something and then stop before you finished?"

"It's what I was talking about before," I said, feeling desperate. "It's the same reason I haven't been afraid of the crabs enough, the same reason I'm so hungry, even though I know they'll eat me when I gain enough weight. Something in my brain is doing it to me, and it also won't let me talk about esca—" I gagged and was cut off before I could even finish the word.

Julian put a claw to his mouth, looking as pale as a crab could look. "Oh, my bloody head spikes," he whispered. "Oh, my darling pictheosaur! I had no idea." And he blinked out of existence.

"What was the matter with *him?*" Katie said. "He ran away before he would even tell us why he was afraid. The jerk!"

But she was scared, too, I could tell. "What did he mean?" I asked, even though I knew Katie didn't know. "He got so upset when I told him about my peculiar behavior. Almost like . . . like he knows what's wrong with me. And he was too afraid to say it!"

17

After our sauna the next day I figured out something even more disgusting about the crabs.

We were always draped in heavy towels in the sauna, even though it was very hot in there and we both sweated profusely. The crabs never went in for very long—they didn't seem to like the intense heat. When the towels were thoroughly soaked with our perspiration, the crab watching us through the glass window in the door would come in and quickly remove the towels and replace them with dry ones, which would then soon become soaked, too, and collected. We had wondered about this a little, but there was so much else on our minds that we hadn't bothered to try to understand it.

But today I noticed, when we left the sauna to head for the mud-pack room and the showers there, that the crab with the latest sweat-soaked batch of towels carried them quickly downstairs in the direction of the kitchen. I felt sick.

I didn't know if the crab guard prodding us along could understand English—none of them spoke much to us except Abamee—but I whispered anyway. "Katie. Now I understand about the towels. I think they're . . . collecting our sweat."

"Huh?"

"I bet they're taking the wet towels down to the kitchen. And wringing them out into a big pot. Saving our sweat. Maybe to use it in . . . some kind of sauce or something. For when they eat us." I remembered one of the things Mom did when she cooked French food. "Maybe so they can boil it down to a concentrate— essence of human sweat. And why are they always cleaning out our ears with those little things like cotton? They do it every time after our facial massage. They're probably saving our ear wax, too, and adding *that* to the sauce. Mmmm. Yum yum."

She looked away from me, frowning. "I don't want to think about it," she said. "All I want to think about is . . ." She glanced over at the crab guard and then said, "You know what I want to think about. And you better be thinking about it, too."

I was. When my mind was clear enough I thought about escape a lot. It was so frustrating! If only the aliens weren't so contentious and hostile, they could get us out of here right away. But not them.

And how long were the lichen going to stay here? How long would it take them to get the slime mold?

And wouldn't they want to get away from the others, to protect The Piggy? What if they had left already? Would we eventually be dragged into an endless intergalactic hunt for them? Or would the aliens decide that since they couldn't agree about getting us out of here, it might be better for them to just follow the lichen? Then we would never be rescued.

But I couldn't tell any of this to Katie now. I had to wait until we were alone.

And finally—after our day of marination therapy and sauna and steam and mud packs and massage, and the usual glass after glass of water to make more sweat—during our free time before dinner I told her.

"But maybe there's still something else the aliens could do," she said stubbornly. She wanted desperately to believe they could.

"We'll just have to wait until Julian comes back, and ask him again."

"Well, he better come soon," Katie said hotly.

It was a struggle for me not to stuff myself at dinner. There was juicily marbled tenderloin of beef baked in a rich puff-pastry crust, and wonderful thick winy brown gravy to ladle over it, and scalloped potatoes with onions and lots of cheese, and vegetables drowned in buttery hollandaise sauce. The food was so enticing, and hunger gnawed at me, and Abamee sat there with his little tentacled eyes following the forks going into our mouths, probably counting every bite. And prodding us to tell stories. And now I understood the function of the stories. They were to distract *us,* to keep *our* minds off our true situation, so we'd overeat without realizing it.

But Katie's eyes were on me, too, unflinchingly. And Katie had more power over me than Abamee did. Despite all of Abamee's sighing, and his urging us to eat more, and his deep sadness and regret that the food was not good enough for us, I forced myself not even to finish the first helping. Katie was tough all right. I was lucky she was with me, and I knew it more than ever now.

In fact we both ate and drank so little that we were not as sleepy as usual after dinner. But we pretended to be. It was Katie's idea, and I caught on when she started yawning in my face. So I began yawning, too, and let my eyelids droop and my head wobble. And finally Abamee gave up and escorted us to our suite and locked us in.

And it was a lucky thing we weren't sleepy, because that evening Julian paid us another visit.

"Haven't lost much weight yet, mate," he said when he appeared.

We were all in the living room. "It can't happen in one day," I said irritably. "And I ate less today than any day since we got here, right, Katie?"

"Yeah, he did," Katie said. "He finally seems to be catching on. Took a while."

"Now I understand why," Julian said. And clapped his mouth shut.

"Well? Why?" I asked him. "You can't say you know what's wrong with me and then not tell me."

"Who says I can't?" he said, and if he'd been in human form, he would have given me that lopsided grin, I knew.

"Look, you're going to have to tell us," Katie said

firmly. "But there's something else we need to discuss. Are the lichen still even here?"

"For some reason, the bloody little devils *are* still here," Julian said. "None of us can figure out why; they should have gathered enough slime mold by now. But they're still hanging around, for some reason. And the others still refuse to agree on all the details of the rescue plan."

Katie's face fell. She turned away, probably to hide her tears.

Julian sighed. It almost seemed again that he cared— and not just about me getting The Piggy for him.

"But the way the lichen are hanging around, even when they don't need to anymore," Katie said. "Maybe it means something—something hopeful."

"It's possible," Julian agreed. "There's just no way of knowing. It seems like a stalemate right now, but we can't let it be. We've got to do something, and fast, too." He turned and looked at me. "Because of . . . because of you, Barney. And the little friend you're carrying."

"What do you mean by that?" I demanded, not sure I really wanted to know.

"Friend?" Katie said.

"A bit of sarcasm, that. 'Friend' is just about the last thing you'd call her. Would you believe, even the others felt a little sorry for you, Barney, when I told them. Of course the main concern of all of us is getting The Piggy—I have to admit that, too, Barney. So now that we know you're compromised, that's our major worry. Still, they felt a little sorry for you. Not as sorry as I am, of course. But more than I'd expect, having gotten to know them."

I felt a very deep chill now. I knew them well. And if they felt sorry for me, then whatever it was that was wrong with me must be something really, really bad.

But I couldn't talk, I couldn't ask him what it was. I could only try to speak, and end up choking again.

Katie understood. "Tell us, please. Even if it's really terrible, we have to know. And you can see that Barney can't ask."

My head was feeling stranger than ever now. There was a ringing in my ears that had never happened before. Even if Julian did talk, I might not be able to hear him. And now I was sure this partial deafness was being caused by exactly what he was about to tell us.

"Creature . . . Toxoplasma . . . parasite . . . brain . . . hormones . . . control . . ."

I watched Katie's face, straining to hear the occasional word through the ringing. And her face grew whiter and whiter as she stared at me, her mouth half-open.

"Reproduce . . . crab . . . goal . . . eaten . . ."

Katie put her hand over her mouth, still staring at me.

"I can't hear you!" I burst out. "Something's wrong with my ears." Even my own voice sounded distant and fuzzy.

They looked at each other and said something, then nodded in agreement. They started talking. The ringing faded away.

"So that's the problem," Julian was saying. "Only Barney can get near the lichen, or even communicate with them. But Barney's imprisoned here. Tricky little situation."

"So we might really *have* to go back to plan A, then,"

Katie said. "With those two aliens in disguise, and you not keeping your promise to the others not to—"

"Shhh!" Julian said instantly. "You have to understand. Barney can't know about it."

"I can't know about it?" I said, feeling left out now along with everything else. "But what's wrong with me?" I begged Julian.

"If I start talking about it, she'll just block it out again," he said. "She doesn't want you to know."

"Who's *she*?"

"Sorry. Can't tell you. I don't know how you're ever going to find out the truth."

I groaned. It was bad enough knowing something was horribly wrong with me—especially here, in the worst situation I'd ever been in. It made it even worse not to be able to know what it *was* that was wrong with me. I tried to piece together the few words of Julian's I had been able to hear. I couldn't do it. The problem in my brain was blocking me again.

"See you later, Barney," Julian said. "Come on, Katie. Barney, you go to your room or we won't be able to talk."

"What? But I *have* to know! I mean, if you're talking about escap—" I choked and gasped for breath.

"That's exactly why you can't hear, Barney," Katie said sadly. She came over to me and put her hand on my shoulder; it was the first time since we had arrived here that she had touched me like that. "It's going to be hard, Barney—really hard. But you have to try. You can't spy on us, or eavesdrop. We know you'll want to. She'll try to make you. But you have to resist. Do *everything* you can to resist. Go to your room. Read. It's our only hope. Do you understand?"

I didn't like what they were asking me to do. But she had touched me. Maybe it was for my own good. "Well . . ." I said stubbornly.

"It's not your fault, and it's not our fault," crab Julian said. "You can't understand, but you have to do what we say anyway. She's already heard way too much, before we knew about her. You go on now."

"But—"

Katie hugged me, then stepped back, her hands still on my shoulders. "Barney," she said, in a gentle tone I had never heard from her before. "For us. You can do it for you and me. I know how hard it will be. But it's our only hope." She took her hands from my shoulders and wiped her eyes, still looking into mine.

I didn't like it. I didn't like it at all. But Katie had never been so intimate with me before. I forced myself, step by inching step, to creep to my room and let them talk in private.

18

Madame Gondii didn't like it either. She *really* didn't like it.

She knew the other two creatures were going to be talking about an escape plan—a strategy of getting Barney away from the crabs. She had listened very carefully whenever they had talked about this before. The more she knew about what they were planning to do, the easier it would be for her to force Barney to resist doing it, and never get away from here.

But now the other creatures knew about her. She had slipped up, letting Barney describe his symptoms to the *Guanophilia lutansia* worm. The worm was an intelligent parasite, too, and he had heard all about her and her life cycle. Now he knew she was inhabiting Barney's brain, and doing everything she could to get him eaten by the crabs as soon as possible.

138

And the horrible worm had tried to tell Barney that she was there inside him, and what she was trying to do to him! She seethed.

Fortunately she had managed to prevent Barney from hearing any of it. The more he consciously knew, the less control she would have over him. So she had poured in deafness hormones to keep him ignorant.

Still, now her problems were worse than before. She had so many things to do all at once! She had to keep modifying her own hormones so that she would live longer than usual, and be able to reproduce longer than usual, in order to wait it out until Barney was fat enough for the crabs. This was not an easy job. It took a lot of time and thought and experimentation with her hormonal mixtures.

When she had first realized she had to do this, she hadn't thought it would be so difficult, because she had been reasonably sure there was no way for Barney to escape. That meant all she had to do was keep him hungry, which was an easy job that did not require a lot of effort. And she would be able to concentrate on modifying herself.

And perhaps that very concentration was what had caused her to slip up, and not stop Barney from describing his symptoms. Now they knew about her. Now they could conspire against her.

She also hadn't factored in how powerful his human friend was. Because of her, he hadn't had a second helping at dinner tonight, he hadn't even finished his *first* helping! Madame Gondii felt like a failure: That girl was more powerful than her own hunger hormones. How could that be? The girl wasn't pumping hormones into

Barney's bloodstream like she was. She wasn't injecting anything into him. So how was it possible for her to counteract Madame Gondii's hormones? She didn't understand it.

Why did human beings have to be so inexplicable, so baffling? It was that same old problem she was always battling with them over. That terrible, destructive thing about sacrifice, about giving up something important to your own life in order to help another individual.

To do so for one's offspring, yes, that she knew deeply. That was primal, instinctive. It was the reason for everything in her life: to get into a crab and be able to have babies.

But this girl was not Barney's offspring. And they weren't mating. Yet he was *still* making sacrifices for her! Madame Gondii would never understand it, never.

And now it was worse than inexplicable, it was interfering with her own plans more than ever before. Her large cauldron, made of her own dried excrement, had to be emptied of the hormones she had been working on to try to prolong her own life cycle. Then, squatting in the cauldron, she excreted from various parts of her body her most potent curiosity hormones. And pain hormones, too—these she added on purpose because of her competition with the human girl. She would beat her! She mixed them together with her many legs into a powerful bubbling froth.

But even as she poured this concoction into the funnel of skin that fed directly into Barney's artery, right there in his brain, he moved step-by-step away from the others into his room. He lay down woodenly on his bed.

He picked up a *book!* He cared about that girl so much that he was obeying *her,* and resisting Madame Gondii's hormones. She wanted to howl with frustration, even as she worked.

Several times Barney started to get up. Madame Gondii *willed* him to go. But he lay back down again. It was very, very hard for him; she knew how her hormones made him feel. And yet there he stayed, despite everything she could do.

And in the other room they were talking about escape. And she couldn't listen! How could this be happening to her?

She wanted to howl, yes, but she was a logical creature. So she kept pumping the hormones. And she also kept thinking.

She knew—from what she had heard before they knew about her—that their ships wouldn't rescue Barney. That was good, very, very good. She was glad she had heard it.

She also knew they had another plan, a crackpot scheme of trying to disguise themselves as crabs and drug the guards and walk Barney and his friend out of the palace. She hoped they would try that, she just hoped they would! Then she'd show them. No way would she let that happen.

There were several things she could do to prevent it. She had believed at first that she could simply make Barney refuse to go. But now she wasn't so sure that would work, because of the peculiar power his feelings for the girl had over him. So she would have to foil the plan in another way. It should be easy enough.

She thought it all out carefully as she kept pouring in the hormones. She could just wipe out Barney's disguise. That would be beyond the girl's control, and Barney's, too. And then the crabs would know what was going on, and eat him faster than ever so that he wouldn't try to escape again.

But now that Barney's friends knew about her, perhaps they also knew a plan like that wouldn't work. And there they were in the other room, discussing it. What were they talking about? Oh, how she longed to know!

And that wretched, wretched girl had so much power over Barney. His whole body was quivering with the effort it took, and yet he was still managing to resist Madame Gondii's hormones, and stay there in bed, looking blindly at the book.

And until Barney got eaten by a crab, Madame Gondii was trapped in the cyst in his brain. What he couldn't see or hear, she couldn't see or hear. And his friends knew it. She had never been more frustrated in her life.

But at least she was prepared now. Prepared so that whatever happened she would be on her guard, and act faster than ever. Knowing what was required of her made her stronger and more determined. She could feel it, she could feel her body reacting to the challenge, and growing more powerful and more alert.

Whatever they tried, she would be able to counter it. Despite everything, she was still sure of that.

It was agony. Never, ever in my life had I been so curious. The desire to know what Katie and Julian were talking about was like a terrible itch over my entire body—an itch that both Katie and Julian had told me I *must not scratch.*

I was on a sickbed, quivering in pain, and there was no medicine to stop it. I picked up a book, but it was no distraction. The pain behind my eyes blurred the words illegibly.

If only, if *only,* I could go in there and listen! More than once I started to get up, and the itching and pain began to abate. And then I remembered the sad warmth in Katie's voice when she told me I must not listen to them, and how she had touched me, and I lay back down again, and back came the terrible itch.

But something else was happening, too. Because so much of this peculiar energy coming from my brain was focused on making me curious, there were other things that it wasn't controlling. Such as blocking out the few words I had managed to hear while Julian was talking about what was wrong with me. I could remember them now. I could try to put them together like a puzzle. And in a way, concentrating on this puzzle actually helped me to resist the urge to eavesdrop on them.

Creature was the first word I remembered, and of course that was easy to understand. The next word, *Toxoplasma,* was hopeless, so I skipped over it. *Parasite* and *brain* both made a lot of horrible sense. So did *hormones* and *control.*

I knew more than I ever had about parasites now. Julian was a parasite, and so were Soma and her offspring. They tortured and killed their host in order to eat and be born. Julian was a lot more benign—though he had admitted that his home in the dinosaur's intestine kept the reptile from growing as it normally would have. In any case, the point was that parasites were everywhere.

Parasite . . . brain . . . hormones . . . control . . .

Had Julian been saying that there was a parasite in my brain, that was using hormones to control me? The idea was so repellent it made me squirm as miserably as the itch I was suffering from. But he *must* have been saying that! It made all the sense in the world. It explained what was happening to me right this minute. Whatever the parasite's eventual objective was, what it wanted right now was for me—and it—to hear what escape plans they were making. And in a certain way, simply knowing that fact was what might be making it possible for me to resist its attempt at control.

The pain wasn't just behind my eyes now. It was creeping down through my bloodstream like fingers of fire. I struggled to concentrate. I was pretty sure that the more I understood, the better I would be able to fight it. I went back to puzzling out what Julian had been saying.

The last set of words were harder: *reproduce . . . crab . . . goal . . . eaten . . . mustn't know . . .*

No matter how hard I tried, I couldn't figure out the connection between *reproduce* and *crab*. All I could guess was that *reproduce* must mean the parasite was female. But *goal* and *eaten* were not quite as difficult. The sentence he actually said might have been something like, "Her goal is for Barney to be eaten."

I groaned, from the miserable itch of curiosity and the fiery pain, but even more from the horror of that sentence. Because what made it so horrible was that it was a perfect explanation for my peculiar behavior.

Everything unnatural I had done must have been the influence of the parasite. It had made me curious about this planet and the crabs from the beginning. It had made me not mind being captured by them. Instead of being terrified, like Katie was, I had been entranced by the beauty of the planet. I had not escaped from the carriage when I had the chance. I had obediently stuffed myself at every meal, and gotten fat. All of these things were bringing me closer to being eaten—unlike Katie, who was resisting like a normal, uninfected person would.

This was a pivotal moment. If I didn't start resisting now—and keep resisting—I *would* be eaten.

It was the hardest thing I had ever done. But now I knew I was fighting for my life. And knowing that kept me from getting up and listening to the escape plan, despite all the pain the parasite was inflicting.

And how had it gotten inside of me anyway? Was it an Earth parasite or an alien one? I figured it had to be an alien one, or else it wouldn't know about the crabs and want me to be eaten by them. And it wasn't hard to figure out how it could have gotten inside of me. It could easily have been planted by Zulma, Moyna, or Jrlb last summer. It was just the horrible kind of thing any of them would do. Julian had said they felt sorry for me when he told them about it, but that was an act. Julian had his naive side.

And then there were the lichen. After all, I had *been* a lichen last summer, by using a disguise selector. I had been right there in the middle of their horrible pink smear of a colony, where they ate everything that came across their path. It would be surprising if something awful *hadn't* gotten into me after my intimate contact with them.

And what was most awful about this parasite was how maliciously she was trying to control me by hurting me—hurting me so that I would get hurt even worse when the crabs ate me. In a way, it was just as bad as Soma's babies eating the living flesh of their helpless suffering host.

And yet . . . here I was, resisting it. Yes, it was hideously painful—the little creature was mightily vicious. But still, I *could* resist it. And simply knowing that resistance was possible made me determined to resist even more.

And to figure out all the answers, too.

They had good reason to ask me to endure this torture, and not listen to them. The parasite could hear what I could hear. And they didn't want her to hear another word about their escape plans. Because if she knew what the escape plans were, then it would be easier for her to prevent us—in particular, *me*—from escaping.

Knowing the reason for it also made me even more determined to go on enduring the torture she was inflicting on me. *So you want to hear? Tough!* I felt like saying. But I didn't say it aloud. I didn't want her to hear those words either. If it was possible, I didn't want her to know I knew about her. I wanted *some* secrets from her, *some* part of my brain that I could call my own. That was worth fighting hard for.

The downside was, *I* wanted to know what the escape plan was, too—it wasn't only her hormones that were making me curious. Everything about this situation was so difficult! In a way, it was worse than fighting the aliens last summer.

Except for one major difference—this time I wasn't alone. I really did believe that Julian wanted me to survive, that he cared what happened to me. Sure, he wanted The Piggy, like they all did. But he didn't want to have to kill me in order to get it. And that was more than I could say about any of the other aliens.

More important, I was with Katie. If she hadn't been here, I might already be fat enough for the crabs to eat. She was literally saving my life.

It was also just so comforting to have her *with* me. I had liked her from the beginning, when we first met at the library. My feelings for her were a lot stronger now.

I was enduring this torture to save my life. I was also doing it because she asked me to. She seemed to know how hard it would be. I was determined to show her that I could do it—that I was stronger than this nasty parasite, and that I would do everything I could to save Katie's life as well as my own.

I had been screwing up until now. I could understand why Katie had been cold, not understanding that it wasn't really my fault, that it wasn't really me screwing up at all. But now that we both *did* understand what was doing it, I wasn't going to screw up anymore. I lay there and trembled as the pain coursing through my bloodstream grew more searing, stared unseeing at the book, and made no more moves to get up. And it went on and on and on.

"Oh, Barney," Katie said, and I looked up to see her standing in the doorway. "Oh, you look *terrible!*" Her eyes reddened and I thought she might cry for real this time.

I got out of bed and hurried over to her. And the pain going away was about one hundred times more wonderful than the feeling you have when you wake up after a long illness and know that you're well again.

Katie squeezed my hand, and we went into the living room, where Julian was. "Curiosity killed the cat, lad," Julian said, after his first look at me. But he didn't say anything about the parasite. I had been right when I guessed that I would be able to fight her better if she didn't know I knew about her.

And Katie was looking at me in a way she had never looked at me before.

"So what's the plan?" I said, without thinking. And then I said, "Oops!" and briefly put my hand over my mouth. "Sorry. It just popped out."

"Are you okay, Barney?" Katie said. "Was it really awful?"

"Yeah," I said, seeing no reason to make light of it. "I don't understand what was the matter with me, but it really felt horrible. Yeah, it must have been the food," I added, continuing the deception. "If the food makes me so sick, maybe I won't have any snacks tonight."

"Good idea, lad. Hope I see you blokes later—in a hundred years, maybe." He gave Katie a look, obviously something to do with their secret plan. And then Julian was gone.

Now that we were alone, Katie might tell me what the escape plan was.

I started to ask her. But before I even started to say it, I stopped myself. I was able to stop because I knew why I was asking. All that came out was a sort of gulp.

But Katie must have known what I was going to ask because she said, "Let's not talk now. I'm exhausted. Have some of that drink from the decanter beside the bed, Barney. Good night." She kissed me lightly on the cheek and went to her room and closed the door.

The next morning I ate less than half my breakfast of fried egg on top of fried ham on top of a toasted buttered English muffin, with hollandaise sauce on top. I barely nibbled at it. Abamee was miserable about it and did everything he could to make me feel guilty. I didn't feel guilty.

"You were wonderful at breakfast, Barney," Katie said

as soon as Abamee had left us alone in the marination therapy pool.

We went through the usual routine—eating, marination therapy, mud pack, massage, steam, sauna, no exercise. But it was not the same today. Katie was not cold and disapproving as she had been ever since we got here. She was warm and friendly. I'll never forget the sight of her smiling at me through the gray mud all over her face, which made her teeth look whiter and her eyes a brighter blue.

Her being so nice made it easier for me to eat practically nothing at lunch. Katie's warmth and approval outweighed Abamee's disappointment by about one million percent.

There was another difference in the way she looked at me. It was not a pitying look, though there was some of that. It was more like she was worrying about me, in a caring way—the way you care about someone very important to you, who has a problem that you can't do anything about, except to be as nice as possible to them. That felt good.

At the same time she was also more tense. Of course she had always been tense and unhappy, ever since we had been captured. But this tension was different. She was stiffer than usual in the marination therapy pool. She flinched more often while we were being massaged, and grimaced more under the mud-pack treatment, when she wasn't smiling at me. She jumped a little whenever Abamee's footsteps came clicking along.

It was as though she was expecting something scary and dangerous to happen at any instant. I tried not to notice. I tried not to think about it. But it was impossible. It was like the ancient alchemists' recipe for turning lead into gold—stir the molten lead while *not* thinking of the word *rhinoceros.*

Though I didn't want the parasite to know anything about the escape plans they had made, I couldn't help being consciously aware that whatever was going to happen, it was going to happen soon.

20

And it did.

As well as being kinder, and more nervous, Katie was also in a more complimentary mood than she had been before we knew about my parasite. She told me several times how strong and brave I was.

Lunch was particularly hard. I was so hungry! And the chef had made a tempting change in the menu, giving us teenage food instead of gourmet—hamburgers, french fries, sausage-and-cheese pizza—the best fast food I'd ever tasted. I gritted my teeth and barely ate a thing. And after lunch Katie said, "You're losing weight already. Thank you, Barney. You're saving both of us. It must be so hard. I know she's making—" she started to say, and then stopped.

She had been about to mention the parasite, but

didn't. And I didn't say anything about it either—though I would have loved to get some extra comfort from Katie about the terrible hunger pangs the parasite was inflicting on me.

Abamee locked us into our rooms, clucking sadly and hoping we would get our appetites back by dinnertime, and telling us with a hint of sternness in his voice how everybody was *very* disappointed in us.

Katie didn't rest, as we usually did after lunch. She paced. She kept sitting down and trying to relax. And then she'd get up again. I wanted to tell her not to do it, that it would give away the fact that something was about to happen, and the parasite would be prepared. But I couldn't.

I was nervous, too—probably more nervous than Katie. At least she *knew* what was going to happen, however risky it might be. But I didn't have a clue. That made it worse. I felt like pacing, too.

But yesterday's ordeal had taught me a lot about control. I was able to sit down comfortably and pick up a book, just as though I had no idea anything was going to happen. I could only hope the parasite would be fooled by this.

Abamee knocked on the door earlier than usual, and Katie jumped more nervously than ever. The locks clicked. "Excuse me," Abamee called, before opening the door. "Do I have your permission to bring in some visiting dignitaries, to observe your quarters?"

"Er . . . just a minute, we'll be ready in a second," Katie called back. "I want to look my best." She hurried into her bathroom.

I tried not to think about it, I tried desperately. But again I couldn't help it. The visiting dignitaries could be Zulma and Moyna, disguised as crabs. And maybe it was part of the plan for Katie to make them wait so it wouldn't seem like we were expecting them.

I could hardly believe they had chosen *this* plan! It was so risky—it hadn't just been the parasite that had made me object to it. Worst of all, the parasite must have heard us discussing this plan. She could know all about it. She might have already made a strategy about how to sabotage it.

But I couldn't object, I couldn't say anything. I just sat on the couch, forcing myself to act calm, even though my heart was racing—and *that* was something the parasite almost certainly would be aware of.

Katie came back from the bathroom, having put on a little makeup. "Okay, ready now," she called out.

Abamee pushed open the door, and then bowed and ushered in two very realistic-looking crabs. They both had some kind of medallions on their arms, just behind the front claws. Had they learned enough about crab culture to know that these medallions had some importance in crab society? I hoped Zulma and Moyna had done their homework.

Abamee followed them in and then locked the door from the inside to make sure Katie and I couldn't get out. He spoke to the two crabs in their own language. They answered him in the same speech.

I could tell Abamee was stressed. He had that funny look around his half-open mouth. I remembered him saying that stress made him ravenous. Surely he wouldn't try to eat me *now*.

Still, he did his best to act normal as he led the two new crabs around the suite, and they scuttled importantly behind him. They studied everything, looking out at the balcony, going into our bedrooms and bathrooms. Abamee talked to them, perhaps explaining why human beings like it this way or that way. The two of them made crab comments to each other, and also seemed to be asking Abamee questions. They were doing a very good job of acting like they really *were* curious about everything. It reminded me of the way they had explored our house last summer.

Katie and I watched them from the couches, both trying to act normal now—though it was only natural that we would be curious about what was going on, since it was so unusual. I kept trying not to wonder when they were going to make their move.

They were in my bathroom when we heard something clattering to the floor like a tower of wooden blocks. The two new crabs came hurrying out into the living room, one of them putting something that looked like a nasty sharp little weapon back into its medallion. The medallions were not just decorative, they were containers. The other one was removing two things like wristwatches from its medallion. I recognized them immediately: disguise selectors.

"What did you do to him?" I asked them. "You didn't kill him, did you? You just knocked him out, right?"

"Whatever are you worried about that crab for? All he wanted was to devour you. Don't be so pathetically *human!* We don't have eons here," one of the crabs said. It was Zulma, speaking in her nasty screech of a voice—but a quiet screech, in this situation. "We're in a vast hurry now. We have to be out of this building before it's time for your next treatment, or they'll know something's wrong." She held out the disguise selectors. "Put these on and depress the button—they're both set on the right species." Katie and I jumped up and she handed them to us. I slipped mine on. Katie looked at hers curiously.

"Just put it on and jam this button right here, the *only* button there is on it, okay, sweetie?" Zulma said sarcastically to her. "Are you dumber than Barney or what?"

Kindly, friendly rescuers they were!

We both put them on and pressed. Instantly everything looked and felt different—alarmingly different.

The crabs had two eyes, like we did. And like our eyes, each one saw a different view of the world. But unlike our eyes, the crab-eye views did not blend together to create three-dimensional vision. What the right eye saw was completely different from what the left eye saw. The whole world was split into a flat left side and a flat right side, with a black gap in the middle. It was extremely disorienting. But it did explain why the crabs walked sideways more often than forward.

It also felt very weird walking on clawed feet. We both lurched around clumsily, bumping into things. We were going to have to try to escape and act like real crabs in completely foreign bodies like these?

"You have fifteen minutess to get your bearingss. We included that in, ssince we knew you'd be sso humanly sslow about it," lisped the other crab, clearly Moyna. "Sso walk around, obsserve the view, hurry! All the other playerss are hidden and waiting nearby."

156

Katie the crab glanced at me for a second. Of course I knew she was hiding something from me. It made me wonder even more if she and Julian had a secret plan that the others didn't know about.

We tottered out onto the balcony and looked at the view. It was like looking at two different sets of mountain ranges. But because I had looked at this view many times, and remembered what it looked like to my own eyes, after a minute or so I could almost put the two pictures together.

"Can you make a little sense out of it now, Katie," I tried to say. It came out as a garbled crackling that was completely unintelligible. So was Katie's emotional answer. The crabs' oral anatomy was very different from humans'—and unlike the lichen, they did not communicate by electronic impulses. Being a lichen last summer had been a *lot* easier.

"Don't even bother to attempt. You're not going to be capable of conversing," Zulma said helpfully. "Your poor little species isn't used to assuming disguises, as we are."

We could hardly see, we could hardly walk, and we couldn't communicate. Great! This escape plan seemed even more dangerously risky than it had when I had first heard it.

But one thing that *wasn't* happening was that the parasite wasn't trying to make me resist it.

I didn't understand. I would have expected the parasite to be inflicting the same kind of pain on me as she had last night, to make it even more difficult, if not impossible, to go along with this plan. But she wasn't. I felt no pain, no resistance at all. It was baffling. What was she waiting for?

But I couldn't waste time wondering about what moment she would choose to hit me with her agonizing hormones. I had to learn how to be a crab, and we had very little time to do it.

Gradually it got easier. We stopped bumping into things. I began to be able to see my way without quite as much difficulty.

"Time'ss up!" Moyna said, way too soon. "We've got to convey you out of here now, before they get ssusspiciouss."

I tried to beg for more time, but of course I couldn't make the words come out.

Zulma knew what I was asking for. "One more minute," she said, relenting, and Katie and I continued to barge around, trying to do it as smoothly and naturally as possible. And Katie *was* beginning to look a lot better. I hoped I was, too.

"Okay, time's really elapsed now, out we go," Zulma said. "You're learning just as lethargically as we expected, but it'll have to do. And don't crack open your mouths to make utterance, no matter what." She unlocked the door with Abamee's keys, which I now noticed she'd been holding, and she and Moyna stepped out into the corridor. We followed very, very hesitantly.

And still the parasite wasn't doing anything to stop me. What was she going to do, and when?

Getting down the stairs was the first major hurdle. Zulma and Moyna did it effortlessly, sideways, just like crabs. But they'd had a lot longer to practice being crabs than we'd had. They'd had the disguise selectors all along and could have been learning how to see and walk for as long as we'd been here. And it didn't help that we'd had almost no exercise for all this time. Katie hadn't gained weight like I had, but she must have lost some muscle tone and coordination. And being crabs was like being trapped in heavy, unyielding armor—which of course was what the crabs' shells really were. Every movement was a conscious effort.

Katie went onto the stairs before me, going sideways, too. I could see how much trouble she was having, and she slipped and almost fell a couple of times, but managed to right herself and prevent any really bad tumbles. Still, it was a good thing no other crabs were around. And I was clumsier than Katie at it—I was fatter and in worse shape, after all. I could feel immediately why the crabs always went sideways on stairs. Because of the way their bodies were shaped, trying to go forward would have resulted in rolling all the way down. And going sideways, because of the way the crab eyes worked, I could see the stairs below me and above me at the same time, to be sure I placed the front and back legs in the right places.

Katie was almost at the bottom now. I slipped, and righted myself, and went a few more steps. I slipped again, and barely managed to get back up, my heart thudding. And then I slipped a third time, and couldn't get a foothold, and down I bumped, all the way down, slamming my undershell on every step, making a terrible clatter. At least it didn't hurt much—the crab shells were thick and tough.

Zulma and Moyna were waiting at the bottom and I could *feel* their rage and disgust. But they couldn't say anything. We could only hope none of the other crabs had heard. It was unlikely, but no one came running, so we just kept on going.

We followed Zulma and Moyna down the corridor, through the mud room, then down another corridor. They had learned their way around this building very quickly, I had to give them credit for that. We were passing other crabs now, but they only bowed slightly to Zulma and Moyna when they waved their medallions at them, and continued going about their business. Soon we were walking past the first atrium. And we reached the front door.

There were no other crabs around at the moment. I saw that Zulma had to make a decision. She could use Abamee's keys, and if she found the right one fast enough, we'd be outside. But if another crab came along while she was using the keys, then the crab would know something was very wrong—why would this visitor have a set of keys? And what about the guards outside? They would see us coming out on our own and they would act.

And so Zulma waited. And that gave Katie and me a little more time to get used to the eyes, the claws, and the armor.

And then a couple of crabs came along. They were carrying towels, so they must have been some kind of maids. Zulma just had time to hide the keys in her medallion. They asked Zulma and Moyna some questions, sounding a little worried. We had no idea what kind of explanation they were coming up with. But, amazingly, it seemed to work. After a short discussion, one of the maid crabs scuttled off sideways and soon came back with a guard, who bowed to Zulma and Moyna, and then said something to us. Zulma or Moyna answered rapidly. The guard thought for a moment. And then it began unlocking the door. There seemed to be a great many locks on it. We waited. This guard didn't seem to be used to opening this door. It was having trouble with the locks, muttering. Someone more important could come along at any moment.

I couldn't believe we were going to make it out of the building so easily. I hated this plan; I was stiff with tension.

And it wasn't because of the parasite, either. She was still leaving me alone. That was beginning to get really frightening. It wasn't like her at all—and I knew her very well by now. She had something up her sleeve, I was sure. And it was going to be something very, very unpleasant; there was no doubt about that.

21

Madame Gondii hadn't felt so unstressed in ages. She scurried back and forth between her window and her kitchen in gleeful anticipation. Soon she would foil all of them, who thought they were so clever; she would ruin their stupid plan to prevent Barney from being eaten and Madame Gondii from getting home and having her babies.

And one of the best parts was that Barney still didn't know about her. She had succeeded in preventing that disaster. She could tell he didn't from listening carefully to all their conversations.

She could sense his crab disguise—she sensed it by how different everything looked to him, and how clumsy he was at getting around. But it felt *nothing* like it would feel for her to be inside a real crab. This was just a cloak, a trick to fool the eyes of those who saw him. She was still inside a human being.

Inside a crab it would be completely different. That was where she belonged. It would be easy, almost effortless, to control a crab brain—not troublesome, as it was to try to control Barney's. She hungered for the luxury and comfort of being home inside a crab.

And it would be soon, very soon. That was a certainty. Now that Barney was in disguise, she could feel how easy it would be to wipe out the disguise, and quickly concocted the mixture. She was just waiting for the right moment—the moment that would be the most painful and disastrous for the humans and the species making this pitiful attempt to help them escape.

The guard was still struggling to unlock the door.

Because Barney was seeing the way a crab sees, Madame Gondii could watch the guard at the door and at the same time watch the interior of the Death Palace behind them. And just as the guard clicked the final lock, Abamee came clattering toward them down the corridor, with three guards armed with crossbows behind him.

Madame Gondii's thing like a heart swelled with eagerness and joy. She wanted Abamee to be here, she wanted him to see everything firsthand. Because he was the one who would decide when Barney was to be eaten. And now he would know Barney and his friends could not be trusted, and that Barney had to be eaten as soon as possible or he'd try to get away again.

The two interlopers disguised as crabs were urging the guard to push open the door. They sounded desperate.

But now the guard wasn't listening. It was looking back at Abamee and the other guards with him.

Abamee came running up to the guard to tell it frantically that the humans had left their rooms. The drug the two "rescuers" had given him had not lasted as long as they expected. Madame Gondii chuckled. They thought they were so smart, but they knew far less about crab—and human—physiology than Madame Gondii did.

Of course Madame Gondii understood the crab language. She had learned it in her infancy, along with her own language. Knowing what they were saying was almost—but not quite—as important as knowing how their bodies worked.

The two interlopers were waving their stupid medallions at Abamee and the guards. A lot of good that would do now! The guards were listening to Abamee. And they were not making a move to open the door. The two interlopers kept trying to interrupt and argue, but they ignored them.

Still, all the crabs were confused. They didn't know about this kind of disguise. They knew something was wrong and that they should not let these crabs out. Now was the time for Madame Gondii to act. She ran into her kitchen and dumped the contents of her cauldron into the funnel that punctured Barney's artery.

It didn't work instantly—she hoped she had done it before it was too late.

And now the guards and Abamee turned to Barney and his horrible friend. They demanded to know what was going on, in crab language. And of course the two disguised humans couldn't say a thing. Madame Gondii was so happy to feel Barney trembling in fear. He would be trembling a lot more in another moment.

And not long after that he would be screaming in agony over the fire. Madame Gondii couldn't wait. She knew the crabs made a point of not cooking the brain— they preferred to eat it raw. She would not be harmed in the fire. And even if it got a little warm, her cyst would protect her. Barney's agony would go on a lot longer than it would have if they *did* cook the brain. When the rest of him was cooked, they would cut off the top of his skull and eat the living neural tissue with special precious-metal spoons, like humans eating thick soup from a communal tureen. She was so impatient for the bliss of that moment!

And also impatient for her disguise-melting hormones to start working. She couldn't wait to see the shock and surprise on all their faces.

It happened. Suddenly Barney could see the way he used to see, he could move the way he used to move. He looked like a human being again.

And they were still inside the Death Palace.

The jaws of all the crabs around him dropped open, those that were disguised and those that were not disguised, displaying their marvelous teeth. For a moment they were all too stunned to move.

Abamee was the first to come to his senses. He cried out an excited order to the guards.

The guard at the door clicked the final lock shut again. And then another. And another.

Madame Gondii danced with joy, feeling young again,

her babies ready to be released. She had foiled the rescue attempt. The humans were still trapped inside the Death Palace. Barney would be eaten very soon!

The two interlopers dropped their disguises. There stood a giant hairy spider, her belly hanging beneath her spindly legs, her spiky teeth almost as impressive as the crabs'. Beside her floated a slimy, veiny, octopuslike thing, with protruding bug eyes and a mouth like a balloon nozzle, brandishing two weapons in the claws at the ends of her suckered tentacles. Both wore breathing gear that hissed rhythmically.

Barney's horrid friend, still in crab disguise, uttered a terrified shriek. It was music to Madame Gondii's things like ears.

Unexpectedly, the crab guard by the door bellowed. Everyone turned to look.

A bubbling pink smear was sliding through the crack under the door. It seemed to have done something to one of the crab guard's claw feet—the crab was hopping away, cradling the injured foot with its other claws.

Madame Gondii's joy dissolved. What was the pink thing? How long was it going to interfere with Barney being eaten?

It was time to release her babies. She had less than an hour to keep them alive inside her.

She had to do something really drastic now.

22

"Katie, drop your disguise! You can fight better without it!"

Crab Katie just stood there, baffled. Streetwise as she was, she had never been in a battle with aliens before. I had.

I reached over and pressed her disguise selector myself. It was a relief to see her as Katie again, even with that terrible expression on her face. Now there was one less crab and one more human. I grabbed her arm and pulled her away from the lichen streaming through under the door. She staggered backward.

Zulma, Moyna, and the four crabs turned toward us. Moyna, the gas bag, brandished two gunlike weapons in the claws at the ends of her suckered tentacles. Zulma's spinnerets throbbed on her fat spider belly, spewing out sticky threads that I knew were as tough as cables. She manipulated the thread with her busy forelegs, ready to heave it at somebody.

But who?

This battle wasn't as clear-cut as the one last summer. Then, Zulma, Moyna, and Jrlb had merely wanted to kill me and get The Piggy. The lichen, and my own smarts, had prevented that. Now there were also Julian, Soma, and the crabs to contend with. If any of the aliens got Katie, they would use her as a prod to control me. None of them would hesitate to kill her, except maybe Julian.

And I had a parasite in my brain.

I pulled Katie backward down the hallway, away from the door and all the other creatures.

An explosion echoed through the building as the doors blasted open. In the instant before I pulled Katie around the corner into the first atrium, Soma glided through the front doors on her gossamer wings, ovipositor at the ready. Lucky for her she could fly—one section of the lichen colony remained spread out in the doorway, preventing all gravity-bound creatures from getting in or out. It was clear from what had happened to the guard's foot that the crabs' shells were no protection from the voracious lichen.

I pulled Katie into the momentary safety of the first atrium. I didn't want her anywhere near that ovipositor. And we knew the layout of the Death Palace better than Soma did.

We both sank down on the benches beside the marination therapy pool, gasping in its soy sauce, ginger, and garlic—with a hint of lemon—aroma. "What's . . . what's going on?" Katie managed to say.

"This is it. We can't sit here for long. Everybody wants me to get The Piggy away from the lichen. They're the pink thing sliming in through the door. Don't let it touch you. And you can't get near any of the others or they'll use you—"

The liquid in the pool boiled and seethed and Jrlb the fish man rose up out of it in his red goggles, his briny reek biting the air. He had no neck or ears, his mouth was a lipless slit, and the three-foot-long sword on his forehead was pointed directly at Katie. I grabbed her arm and dragged her out of the atrium, back into the corridor, heading away from the front door. How were we ever going to get out of here?

"How did it get in there?" Katie said, slightly behind me.

"He has the hyperspace card, remember? You know what that means—he can be anywhere in an instant. But he has to keep going back to water to breathe." We darted into the next atrium, the mud room. "Maybe we can rest here for a minute and try to figure out what to do."

I felt hopeless. Everybody wanted us. And somehow I had to find out what the lichen were doing here, and get The Piggy away from them, *without* letting anyone but Julian know I had it. I would have to offer Julian The Piggy in order for him to get us off this planet and take us home. "How am I going to go into the lichen colony?" I said, and groaned. "Somebody will take you. Soma will lay her eggs in you. It's hopeless!"

Of course there had been plenty of time for me to tell Katie everything that had happened last summer—she knew all about my trip into the lichen colony. She squeezed my hand and then let go of it, shook her head, and pushed back her hair. It was longer now—before it hadn't covered her ears, and now it hung an inch below them. "I can take care of myself," she said. "You do what you have to do, Barney."

"Great," I said sarcastically. "With everybody there is around here trying to get us first."

"But Barney, we have to *try*," Katie said. "We can't give up hope. That's what she—" She stopped herself before mentioning the parasite. But she was right. That's exactly what the parasite in my brain would *want* me to do—give up hope and get caught by the crabs.

Footsteps ratcheted toward us. "Here they come," I said. "We've got to hide somewhere."

"The steam room," Katie whispered. "The crabs don't like it in there."

We hurried out into the corridor, turned left, and pulled open the heavy wooden steam-room door, with its little misted window. Heat blasted us. We pulled the door quickly shut behind us. We left the lamp off so they couldn't see inside.

A moment later we heard the brittle sound of Abamee and the three guards rushing past. We were safe from them, for a short time anyway. We could relax on the wooden bench in here.

In the intense heat. And the steam so thick in the un-lit room we could barely see each other. It would have been a lot pleasanter out in the cool, bright atrium.

"We have to have a strategy," Katie said. I could see her just well enough to know that she was sitting up straight, tense and alert, ready for action.

I still felt hopeless. I shrugged. "Yeah. Sure." I could

already feel my light pajamas clinging to me; my skin was dripping sweat.

Katie sighed. "Pull yourself together, Barney. I can't do this alone. Remember, you beat them last summer. Okay, this time it's more complicated. But now there's two of us."

"But they all have weapons and attributes. We don't have anything."

"You're immune to the lichen," she reminded me. "Nobody else is." She thought for a moment. "You wondered why the lichen are staying down here, instead of running away with The Piggy. There can only be one possible explanation."

"Yeah?" Suddenly she seemed more on top of everything than I was, despite my experience. I was glad she was around to help. But I also felt kind of stupid. "What explanation?"

"The Piggy." Through the steam I could see her wiping sweat out of her eyes with the wet hem of her pajama top. "The lichen wouldn't be here in the Death Palace unless The Piggy wanted them to be here. You said it was always curious, wanting to experience and record new species. It's been with the lichen a long time. Maybe it wants to move on to somebody else now."

"Fine." I was feeling completely negative. "But we already know it doesn't want us—it was with me last summer. It's done the human race already." Sweat was stinging my eyes, too. I tried to wipe it away with the sleeve of my pajama top, which was already wringing wet. "So it wants to experience some other species. That's not going to help us get it and get outside."

"What's the matter with you? Oh! It must be the—anyway, you can still go into the lichen colony and try to get it away from them. That's what you have to do. And the sooner the better."

"What about you? If *any* of the others get their hands on you, we're done for. Then they'll be able to control me and force me to do whatever they—"

The steam-room door swung open and banged against the bench, just missing my leg. Abamee stood there, with the three armed crab guards, holding their cross-bows and wearing quivers of arrows.

Katie and I both squeezed back into the corner, even though we knew there was no way out.

"Go away! The others will get you!" Katie shouted threateningly at them.

"How did you find us?" I stupidly asked, feeling relief that at last this was coming to a conclusion. But that couldn't be my real feeling; it had to be the parasite.

"The incomparable aroma of human perspiration," Abamee said rapturously. "Now come along, my sweet children. Once you are eaten, those other creatures will have no reason to stay here and plague us anymore."

In the next instant we were each being held by two crabs. They had not been prepared for this and weren't wearing gloves; their serrated claws bit painfully through the thin dripping fabric of the pajamas.

Out into the hallway they ran, around several corners. And then down—down to the kitchen and the grilling chamber.

Katie was screaming. "No! No! You can't do this! Help us, somebody help—"

One of the crabs jammed something that looked like a

large used handkerchief into her mouth and held it there.

Down into the corridor with stone walls. Through the metal door into the soundproofed room with the giant fireplace. It was as hot in here as in the steam room; there was a gray ash coating on the charcoal and it was glowing red inside, perfect for slow grilling. They quietly clicked the metal door shut behind us. We could scream our heads off in here and no one would hear.

Now I felt like screaming and struggling. I had put on this act before, pretending I wanted to escape when I really didn't want to. And in the carriage when my feet came loose, I had hidden that from the driver. Clearly the parasite wanted me to be eaten—and just as clearly she didn't want the crabs to know that. Why? Why did the parasite want me to pretend to try to get away?

I remembered how Abamee had watched us so carefully when we were first brought into the courtyard of the Death Palace. The parasite had made me struggle the hardest then—though moments earlier she had prevented me from trying to escape. And after Abamee had watched us struggle he had said, "You have passed the test. You are clean of infection."

Could it be that if I didn't struggle, the crabs would know I was infected, and would not want to eat me?

That was a novel idea. But suddenly it made all the sense in the world.

The parasite wanted me to be eaten by a crab—that was the only explanation for the peculiar way I had been behaving. And if the parasite wanted to get into a crab, that must mean it was part of her natural life cycle. If the parasite and the crab had evolved this way, it had to have happened many times before. The crabs were smart—they would have learned about this parasite and knew they had to be on the lookout for it. That's why the parasite wanted me to put on the act of struggling.

And if I *didn't* struggle, the crabs would know I was infected and therefore not fit to eat. And they wouldn't eat me.

If Katie didn't struggle, they wouldn't eat her either.

"You're not ready yet, I'm sorry to say," Abamee was telling us as they laid us out on the two wheeled tables in preparation for being manacled onto the grill, already so close to the grill that I could feel it painfully hot on my skin. "Especially not you, my poor, thin little girl. But we must do it now so that those awful creatures will leave us alone. Now just try to be good children and accept the inevitable."

"Sure," I said brightly, fighting the parasite's impulse to writhe and scream. "I'm ready. You've kept us waiting long enough." The parasite slapped me with pain. But I had fought her before, in a far less dangerous situation, and I could fight her now. It was doubly important to make it clear that I wanted to be eaten, because maybe then Katie would catch on and put on the same act to save herself.

All four crabs turned and looked at me, their mouths open—but not with hunger.

"I tried to eat as much as possible, just like you wanted. Katie didn't because she didn't understand—until now. But now she knows this is our true destiny. The sooner you eat us the better. Right, Katie? Tell them that's what you really want. Not like those dumb girls before us, who didn't understand. This is our fate. Right, Katie? Come on. Tell them."

"Huh?" she said, baffled. She looked over at me.

I met her eyes and nodded, hoping it was imperceptible to the crabs. "Katie's sorry now she didn't eat very much," I went on. "But she *did* do all the marination therapy and everything. She's glad you're going to eat her now. Tell them, Katie."

She still didn't say anything. But she wasn't struggling now either.

"Come, come," Abamee said, trying to sound businesslike. But there was an uncomfortable edge to his voice. "You don't know what you're saying."

"You didn't know my feet came untied in the carriage on the way here," I said. I was sweating, not only from the heat of the fire, but from the parasite's brutal stinging. But still I persisted, liking this game very much now. "My feet came untied and I could have gotten out of the carriage and run, but I didn't. Because I knew. Something in me wanted this to happen all along. Something small, but very powerful. That's why we came to this planet in the first place."

Katie's mouth fell open. We didn't have ESP, but I could almost *feel* her beginning to understand. And then she said, "Barney's right. I was confused before. But now I know the best thing is for you to eat me, too. That's why I wanted to come here with him, to your beautiful planet. I hope I'll taste good, even though I'm so skinny."

"How did you know anything about the two girls before you?" Abamee demanded, sounding very worried now.

"We snuck down here and watched, when you left us at dinner on our first night here," I explained. "We were so eager and curious to see. We felt sorry for them that they didn't understand, and made so much trouble for all of you. But we won't be like that. We're ready."

Behind the four crabs I saw the pink smear oozing underneath the metal door to this room. I didn't realize the lichen could move so fast. I did my best not to react at all.

Were they after the crabs, or Katie?

"If you're so ready, then why did you disguise yourselves and try to escape today?" Abamee wanted to know.

"That wasn't our fault," Katie said. "Those horrible creatures made us do it. They threatened us with their weapons. We had no choice. Luckily you saved us in time."

The crabs had let go of us. Nothing was holding us to the wheeled tables. But we didn't try to run or even sit up.

"What are you waiting for?" I said sharply. "Hurry up and put us on the grill!"

Nobody was in control of me now, not even the parasite. The expressions on the crabs' faces were worth putting up with all the searing pain she was inflicting on me.

One of the guards roared and jumped up into the air. It roared again when it landed. And then they were all shrieking as the lichen oozed over their clawed feet.

The lethargy and depression I felt only a short time before was gone. I was rejuvenated at having put this over on the crabs. And in fact I wasn't putting anything over on them—I really *was* infected. I had been protecting them.

What was wonderful was that they believed the lie about Katie.

I jumped off the table. My bare feet landed squarely in the middle of the puddle of lichen. The lichen died and crunched under my feet.

Katie started to get off her table, too.

I shook my head at her. "Don't move!" I mouthed. The wheels of the table were metal and therefore impervious to the lichen. I pulled Katie's table over to the door, kicked it open, and pulled her out of the grilling chamber. The lichen were still tormenting the crabs inside. I couldn't help feeling a little bit sorry for Abamee. But he *had* been about to kill us.

There was a wide lapping puddle of lichen out in the hallway, too, I was glad to see. They had ignored the loaded crossbow dropped out there by one of the guards. I picked it up and handed it to Katie, leaving her parked right in the center of the lichen pool.

"Stay here, in the middle of the lichen," I told her. "Then nobody can get near you except Soma and Moyna. If the lichen move, roll your cart along with them. And if you catch a glimpse of Soma or Moyna, kill them with the crossbow."

She examined the crossbow carefully. "It looks like . . . you just pull the trigger right here," she said. She looked up at me. "Are you going into the lichen colony?"

"Yeah. I've got to find out why they're here—and whether or not they brought The Piggy with them." I was still wearing the disguise selector. I activated the display until the lichen appeared on the little screen.

And then I thought of something. It had to be the parasite who had destroyed my crab disguise—she was smart, and had done it right at the worst possible moment. No one else had the control over me to do anything like that. Which meant that she could also prevent me from becoming a lichen if she wanted. Or she could let me go into the colony, and then wipe out my disguise whenever she felt like it.

But maybe if I went into the colony right here, next to the grilling chamber, she'd leave me alone. This is where she wanted me to be—she might still be hoping the crabs would eat me.

We could hear the crabs in the grilling chamber bellowing and yelping from the pain of the lichen—the lichen who were still attached to their colony out in the hallway.

I had to risk going into the colony, whatever the parasite was going to do. I pressed ACTIVATE.

I was a lichen again.

As soon as I entered the colony, I knew what was making me immune—and the terrible price I had to pay for it.

The knowledge was flowing into me from every lichen cell. I hadn't been aware of it last time I was here. Maybe they hadn't either. But this time I had experienced a lot more before I had entered the lichen colony, and they had, too. Now I could feel clearly the underlying physiological data they were relaying to me.

The parasite in my brain was what made me immune to the lichen.

I remembered the marble-sized immunity pill I had swallowed back in the beach house that rainy night last summer. It must have contained the parasite, in some dormant form. She had come to life inside my body, traveled in my bloodstream to the brain, and stayed there. In my brain, she could feed chemicals into me that controlled my behavior.

And these same chemicals—for purely biophysiological reasons—also made me immune to the lichen.

Too bad the game hadn't warned me what immunity really meant; if it had, I wouldn't have taken the pill. But the game wasn't exactly fair. And neither was the entity that ran the game, the entity that manipulated all the species to give it what it wanted—the entity that had directly infected me with the parasite, without warning me.

The Piggy.

Now the information that being lichen immune also meant having a parasite in your brain had probably appeared in my Interstellar Pig rule book. Now that it was too late.

The lichen were talking to me.

"Hey, wake up! Move along with everybody else."

"What's your problem, anyway?"

"No. Don't tell us! We don't want to know your problem. Just move along."

I followed orders and moved along, not knowing yet exactly where we were going.

As before when I'd become a lichen, I did retain some human senses. Part of me could still "see" the Death Palace, and Katie on her table in the middle of our colony.

And, also as before, I felt a powerful hunger.

Lichen hunger was not like crab hunger. The crabs were very particular about what they ate—I knew that from firsthand experience! The lichen just ate—whatever their bodies would ingest. At our rented beach house they had not eaten the linoleum or the vinyl carpet. They seemed to crave natural food—it didn't matter what the food tasted like, it just mattered that it was organic. And there were plenty of microscopic living organisms all over this floor. We gobbled them up as we oozed along.

"Come on, hurry!"

"We need your help, and we don't have much time."

"You need my help?" I asked the lichen, surprised. "Do you know who—what—I am?"

"We know that you are the only organism that can get close enough to us to communicate."

"And the only organism that can get The Piggy away from us."

"Hurry! There isn't much time!"

"What?" I asked them, hardly believing it. "You don't *want* The Piggy?"

"We don't know your units of time."

"But as we measure time, in 437 *nalika* The Piggy is going to make a very large nuclear explosion."

"The game is a lie," another lichen informed me. "It is the species that *has* The Piggy that will be destroyed."

"It will stay here and blow us up unless you forcibly take it away."

"Why else do you think we came here with it?"

"Hurry! We're getting closer!"

They sure were bossy! But I could live with that. I tried to control my excitement so the lichen wouldn't notice it. This was almost a miracle. But it also made perfect sense.

Last summer, The Piggy had told *me* that it was about

to explode, when it had grown tired of being in my possession, and wanted to move on and experience what it was like to be a lichen. And that was why I had told the lichen where I had hidden it.

And then it hadn't exploded after all. But I wasn't going to tell the lichen *that!*

I checked to see what was going on outside. The crabs still seemed to be trapped in the grilling chamber. Katie remained safely on her table in the middle of the lichen colony, alert, looking around her, holding the crossbow at the ready. None of the other creatures had found her in the few seconds I'd been gone. We weren't moving away from her—the lichen around me were simply dragging me toward another place within the lichen colony, a place that was thicker with lichen.

The place where The Piggy must be.

Consume, consume, consume! whirred a bland mechanical voice in the back of my brain. *To eat is to breathe, to eat is to breathe. Oh, our luscious slime mold. But there is plenty to eat in this place, too!*

I recognized The Piggy immediately. It had to be quoting the lichen. The fact that I could hear it at all meant that it was once again in my possession.

Is it true, Piggy? I thought at it. *Are you tired of the lichen now? Where do you want to go next?*

Still waters run deep, The Piggy observed. *Future Librarians of America, 2, 3.*

Typical. It wasn't answering me. It was quoting from the yearbook where I had hidden it last summer.

The Piggy didn't issue orders, it didn't tell the species directly what it wanted—except when it had gushed to me about wanting to experience the lichen. But that was unusual. Generally it worked by lies and trickery—and avoiding direct questions by quoting meaningless stuff it had learned from whatever had possessed it before.

Suddenly I was furious.

I wasn't scared of The Piggy anymore. I hated it now. It had created the game to make all the creatures want it. It didn't care that the game also created hatred and fear, treachery and bloodshed, misery of every kind. All The Piggy cared about was being entertained—at whatever cost to the species it used to entertain it.

I stifled this thought. I stifled the next idea I had. I couldn't let myself think it directly. But now I knew what I wanted to do. It was dangerous; I would be putting Katie and me at greater risk than ever. But I wanted to do this more than anything.

We approached The Piggy. The lichen cells parted just ahead of me. And there was the pink spherical object with its one eye and its idiotically smiling mouth. I felt the sizzling jolt I always felt upon seeing it. I felt disgust. But this time, more than anything else, I felt rage.

I did everything I could to hide it. Fighting the parasite had taught me a lot.

The parasite! She could drop my disguise at any second. I might not have much time.

Piggy, please! What species do you want to experience next? It had told me this last time, when it wanted to go to the lichen. That gave me hope it might tell me now. I had to know where it wanted to go so I could plan my strategy.

Yes, slime mold is our staple, and of course we love it, and take it with us wherever we go, The Piggy replied. *But we also relish the rich succulence of fatty animal flesh, which is most easy for us to catch and subdue at home. Come with us and savor.*

Piggy, I promise you I will leave you with the lichen forever if you don't answer my question, I thought at it as firmly and emphatically as I could. *What species do you want now?*

A crab! The Piggy finally admitted, its voice speeded-up and higher-pitched because of its mechanical excitement at the idea. *A crab afflicted by the Toxoplasma Gondii parasite.*

That had to be my parasite—the parasite that wanted to get into a crab. No wonder The Piggy had tried to avoid telling me! The only way a crab could catch the parasite was by eating *me.* So that's what The Piggy wanted.

I'm going now, and leaving you here, I told it, almost meaning the words. *Do you think I want to let one of them eat me? Anyway, they* know *about the parasite now. They don't* want *to eat me anymore.*

I see. You deduced about the parasite and let the crabs know you have it so they will not eat you. Clever. But there might *be another way . . . Pep Club, 1, 2, 3. Student Council, 3.*

I felt like screaming at it. *Well? Is there another way or isn't there?*

My hyperspace card is the opposite of the one in what you call the game. It is my strength and also my limitation.

And that was all it said. With one million things happening around me, and no time at all, and the parasite still able to wipe away my disguise in an instant—it was expecting me to solve riddles? I cursed it inwardly, but that wasn't doing any good. I had to think—fast.

So its hyperspace card was the opposite of the one in the game. What were the rules of the one in the game? You could use it to take yourself anywhere in an instant. *But you couldn't move anybody else.* I had found that out when I asked Julian if Jrlb could use his hyperspace card to rescue us from the Death Palace.

So the opposite of that would be what? That you could move *other* creatures anywhere in an instant, but not yourself.

Again, excitement was overcoming my frustration. The Piggy could not move itself—that was why it depended on other species, such as me, to move it from one species to another.

But it *could* move other creatures.

Which meant that it could put the parasite into a crab brain *without* the crab having to eat me. Then I would be safe—from the crabs, anyway. And The Piggy would think it was going to get what it wanted. And have me give it to a crab. But I could really do what *I* wanted.

If I could trust The Piggy.

Are you trying to say that you can put the parasite into a crab's brain? Without the crab eating me? And then I can give you to the crab so you can have the experience of an infected crab? Is that the truth?

We are all in the gutter, but some of us are looking at the stars, whirred The Piggy in its normal voice. *Pen in Hand, 1, 2, 3. Editor, The Literary Light, 3.*

It was quoting from the yearbook again. It wasn't going to tell me any more. And I didn't know if I could trust it or not. I could only hope I had really convinced the crabs that it was not safe to eat me.

I flattened my lichen self over The Piggy. With my human vision I touched DEACTIVATE on the disguise selector.

And then I was Barney again, crouching in the middle of the pool of lichen with The Piggy in my hand. I immediately slipped it into the pocket in my pajama pants.

"Not so fast, Barney!" screeched a voice like the sound of a car's brakes just before a crash. I swiveled around, still in a crouch.

Zulma, the bloated spider lady, had arrived. She stood just clear of the puddle of lichen, in a desperate position that required fast action. Her weapon was pointed directly at Katie. Katie's crossbow was pointed directly at Zulma. It was a stalemate—for the moment.

"Your little friend will be charred atomic dust if you don't give The Piggy to me *now!*" Zulma ordered. She laughed, worse than fingernails on a blackboard. "That archaeological weapon of hers is so much tardier than mine."

I scurried into the grilling chamber, pretty sure Katie wouldn't let down her guard and wouldn't pay attention to Zulma's lies.

The lichen were already flowing out of the room, running away from The Piggy. The crabs lay on the floor, exhausted by pain. The lichen hadn't actually eaten them—they didn't seem to like the shells of hard-shelled crabs—but they had gnawed holes in their carapaces, tormenting them to the point that they were beyond chasing me, beyond eating me, beyond doing anything but lying there and moaning.

I grabbed a quiver of crossbow arrows that one of them had dropped on the floor and slung it over my shoulder. I had to do something before the lichen were all gone, and looked quickly around. The room was full of kitchen equipment. I grabbed a metal ladle, squatted at the door, and let the lichen stream into it on their way out, dumping them into a metal bowl every time the ladle filled. I wanted to get back out in the hallway and help Katie, but I needed some lichen first.

"What's he doing in there?" Zulma's screech seemed a little closer now. "Too late, my girlie. Time for you to—"

I heard a whoosh and then a disgusting squishy plunk, followed by a brief piercing shriek that almost made me drop the ladle and put my hands over my ears. The bowl was full of living lichen. I darted outside, still carrying the ladle.

Katie sat upright, on her knees on the table, looking very pale and very scared. Zulma lay on the floor in front of her. The crossbow sure packed a punch—the arrow had entered Zulma's fat belly and gone all the way through her. The tip protruded from her backside. She wouldn't give us any more trouble now.

I grabbed Katie's hand with my one free one. She had saved both our lives. "Barney," she said weakly. "I did it. And I watched her die."

"You had to kill her," I told her. "She would have killed you if you didn't. Let's get away from here now."

"Did you get The Piggy?" she asked me. "Julian wants it."

I put my finger to my lips and nodded.

The lichen weren't even pausing to nibble at Zulma's freshly killed body as they rippled past her—they were in a tremendous hurry to get as far away from The Piggy as possible, now that I had relieved them of it.

The Piggy seemed to have convinced them that only I

could transport it away from them. I was the one The Piggy wanted to be eaten by a crab, after all. Did I really believe that it would use its hyperspace card to get the parasite out of my brain and into a crab? I was sure it would prefer to experience what it felt like for the crab to eat me.

But the crabs no longer seemed to want to eat me, even if they had been strong enough to do it right now.

The lichen slimed away from the floor underneath us. Katie jumped off the table. Unfortunately, Zulma had fallen directly on top of her weapon. We tried to roll her body away to get it, but she was just too heavy, and we had to hurry. We gave up and started to run for the stairs.

I felt a strange sensation behind my right eye, and stopped, and put my hand to my head. And then I ran back and looked into the grilling chamber.

Abamee lay there weakly, one scarred claw just underneath his right eye. "Did you feel something funny, too?" I asked him.

He nodded weakly.

It really seemed to have happened. The Piggy *had* used its special hyperspace card to get the parasite out of my head and into Abamee's.

I hardly dared to believe it was possible. And yet I felt so different that I knew it had to be. Abamee had never looked so repellent—and I had no curiosity about him at all. J'koot no longer seemed beautiful; the whole idea of it was a nightmare. My deepest attitudes toward the crabs and J'koot had changed. All I wanted was to get away from them and never see them again.

The change could only mean one thing.

I was free of the parasite.

The Piggy hadn't done it out of kindness, of course. It did it because it had no other choice if it wanted to get into an infected crab. The Piggy must have been able to sense that Abamee was in no condition to eat me now. And The Piggy was impatient.

I didn't want to think about how Abamee was feeling, or what the parasite might be doing to him.

I knew The Piggy wanted me to give it to Abamee now. That's why it had done this. And when it became clear that I wasn't going to give The Piggy to Abamee, it could also put the parasite back inside me again. I needed to act fast, before it did that. It hardly seemed possible to do all we had to do so quickly, but we had to try.

Without the parasite, I was also no longer immune to the bowl of living lichen in my hand. They would eat through me if I let them touch me. They were surging around a little, but didn't seem to be crawling out of the bowl toward my hand. Maybe they didn't realize I wasn't immune—yet. But as soon as they caught on, they would want to devour me.

"Come on. Upstairs," I told Katie.

"What about all the other creatures up there, wanting to kill us to get The Piggy?"

"We'll lie. We'll tell them I gave it to the crabs." Maybe I should have lied to Katie and told *her* I gave it to the crabs, too, but I didn't want to.

"But how are we going to get out?" she whispered as we hurried quietly up the stairs. "If the other aliens aren't guarding the door, the crabs will be. And some of the lichen might still be at the front door, too."

Katie stopped on the stairs. She frowned. Then she gulped, and started climbing again. "I . . . I have another idea. It's kind of risky. It all depends on how alert Julian is."

"What idea?"

"Come on—it's the only way out of here. And just because the crabs in the grilling room didn't eat us, that doesn't mean the other ones won't. They'll eat me, anyway. I don't have a parasite."

"Neither do I, now," I told her.

She spun around. "What happened?"

"The Piggy put it into Abamee through hyperspace. It wanted to be inside an infected crab. The Piggy was too impatient to wait for Abamee to eat me."

"Barney, that's . . ." She hugged me, carefully, because of the bowl of lichen I was holding. She quickly stepped away. "We have to hurry. I just hope Julian's watching."

We started up the stairs again. What did she have in mind for getting out of here? I was afraid to ask.

We turned at the landing and saw Moyna floating at the top of the stairs, her weapon pointed directly at us. "Well, well, where'ss our old friend Zulma? Have you done me a boon and disspenssed with her already?" She hung there, an octopus with veins and mucus, pulsing like an exposed internal organ. And even down here on the landing we could smell her fetid breath with every word she said.

Katie hadn't thought to put a new arrow in the crossbow. As soon as she moved to do that, Moyna would shoot.

Or maybe she'd shoot anyway.

"Did you conversse with your little friendss the

lichen?" Moyna wanted to know. "Did you asscertain why they are here, and where iss The Piggy?"

"I gave The Piggy to the crabs. That's what it wanted. It was tired of the lichen and threatened to blow them up if they didn't bring it down here so I could give it to the crabs." I rattled out the words, hoping I sounded convincing. Most of what I was saying was the truth—except for the important part.

Moyna rolled her bug eyes at me. I remembered that she was the most gullible of the aliens from the summer. "The crabss? Which crab?" The tentacle with the gun pointing at me didn't flinch.

I stank with sweat, even up here away from the grilling room. "Abamee. He's the fattest one, with the biggest mouth, and orange on his shell. The one you drugged in the bathroom. You can't miss him. He's in the room with the huge fireplace. First door on your left down there." I pointed behind me.

And I wondered: Would Abamee be better off being killed quickly by Moyna, or staying alive to endure whatever the parasite was planning for him?

"And Zulma'ss *dead!*" Moyna crowed in utter delight, peering down the stairs. She swooped below, too impatient to get to The Piggy to pause to shoot us. "You're next!" she howled.

I poured a ladleful of living lichen from my bowl directly onto her head as she went by.

Moyna wasn't expecting *that!* The lichen immediately ate through the gas bag of her head that kept her afloat. As the hydrogen gushed out, she spun down onto the steps, going flat as a pancake almost immediately. We got out of the way fast as she thrashed her clawed tentacles in agony, emitting a high-pitched breathy wail that almost made you feel sorry for her. The lichen swarmed hungrily all over her, stuffing themselves.

We had very little time. In a minute The Piggy would put the parasite back inside me.

Katie fitted another arrow into the crossbow and we headed up to the first floor.

At the top I turned for the front door. "No, Barney," Katie whispered. "That won't work. This way." She kept going up the stairs, to the second floor, where our suite was.

"What are you going up there for? The door's down here!" I whispered back.

"I told you, we can't get through that door. There's crabs there, and lichen, and you're not immune to the lichen anymore. I have another idea."

"Well, what is it?" I wanted to know.

"Better not to know. There's only one way out."

Only one way out? And upstairs? I still had no idea what she was talking about. But I trusted her judgment. She had been right about everything from the beginning. And she had killed Zulma.

Where am I? I do not feel myself in the possession of an infected crab.

In just a minute. Just wait one minute and then you'll have everything you want, I thought at The Piggy, praying that it would believe me. *I've always told you the truth before.*

It said nothing.

Just as we were reaching the top of the stairs, Jrlb flashed out of nowhere, directly above us, his lasso whirling. Katie was too surprised even to aim—and in an instant the lasso was tightening around her. She fell to the floor, dropping the crossbow, completely helpless.

Jrlb's sword whipped across my forehead. I felt it scrape through the skin to the bone. Blood came trickling out. He lowered his head. Now it pointed at my jugular.

I couldn't risk getting close enough to him to drop a ladleful of lichen on his head, and I was too distraught to think clearly. I hurled the entire innocuous-looking bowl at him.

He didn't even flinch away from it or lift his hand to push it away. Lichen splattered all over his face.

Moyna's wail was nothing compared to Jrlb's gurgling roar. The floor reverberated. Every creature in the building would hear it, and know we were up here. Jrlb disappeared instantly, back into the water. Would the lichen mind being underwater? I didn't know. If they drowned, Jrlb would be back.

And now I had no lichen left to fend off anybody else. And there were still Soma and the other crabs. Lots of crabs. And I was healthy now.

"Hurry up! Get me out of this!" Katie demanded.

One minute is up. I still do not feel myself in the possession of an infected crab. The Piggy's voice was as bland as ever.

I ignored The Piggy and pulled the lasso loose from around Katie's arms. In seconds she was up. She grabbed the crossbow and we ran for the door to our suite.

Katie paused an instant before touching the doorknob. Had Zulma locked it? Neither of us could remember. If she had, we'd have to go all the way back down to the basement to get the keys—and it was highly unlikely we'd ever make it back up here again.

Katie turned the knob. The door opened. We both breathed a sigh of thanks to Zulma for being so sloppy.

But I still didn't know what we were doing here. "Katie! We're just running into a place where there's no way out. We're sitting ducks here!"

I had never seen Katie look so pale. "We've got to do this, Barney," she said, barely audibly. "And we've got to do it now, before anybody else gets here and stops us. Come on." She paused and looked up. "Julian. Julian, I hope you're ready."

She pulled open the balcony door. Then, stepping back to stand well inside the room, she aimed and fired the crossbow at the screen that enclosed the balcony. The arrow went right through it and stayed aloft for many yards before turning downward and heading into the chasm.

And now I finally understood. "You want to *jump?*" I shouted at her. "You think Julian will see us and beam us up to his ship before we die?" I shook my head wildly. "You're *crazy!* I'm not doing it. If he thought he could do that, why didn't he say it before?"

I could tell she was as scared as I was. "My hope . . . my hope is that he didn't suggest it before because we had no way of getting through the screen. Now we do." She paused, breathing heavily. "Barney, Julian and I had a secret plan. I couldn't tell you before because of the parasite. Julian was going to defy the others and beam us up to his ship as soon as we got out the front door, and then zoom away from them. Now the others are dead, except Soma. But we can't go through the front door—neither of us realized that would happen. And he *must* be keeping an eye on what's going on down here. He wants The Piggy. This is the only way."

"Katie. The risk is just too huge. He's watching the front door, not the balcony. It's . . ."

I remember when a member of Jrlb's water-breathing species did not obey me, The Piggy whirred blandly. *It did not enjoy thrashing to death in the middle of a desert. That was quite an interesting sensation.*

"What are you two maggots crawling around up here for?" a deep female voice said from behind us.

We spun around. Soma, wings fluttering, hanging in the air, her ovipositor pointed directly at Katie. "Barney. Regurgitate The Piggy. Now," she ordered.

We both backed out onto the balcony. "I gave it to the crab. To Abamee. That's what The Piggy wanted. Down in the grilling chamber. The big fat crab with orange on its shell. That's where—"

"You don't think I can taste the lie in your voice? I crave The Piggy now, or else your little friend will be giving excruciating birth to my litter after several extremely unsavory months of being slowly digested alive."

"Julian! *Catch us!*" Katie screamed, and jumped through the hole in the screen.

I had no choice. I jumped, too.

The Death Palace shot above in an instant. Rock walls flashed past as we fell into the chasm.

And fell.

And kept on falling.

Blackness. And then we were in Julian's E.-coli-stinking ship. Nothing had ever smelled so good.

We both collapsed to the floor. "Oh, thank you, thank you for seeing us in time," Katie managed to moan.

"I bloody well almost didn't!" came Julian's voice from the dinosaur, which seemed to be asleep in its heaped-up pile of excrement. "My robots were watching the front door, as we agreed. It was just chance that one of them looked around to the back as you were falling. I never *imagined* you'd try a stunt like that!"

"Katie. You were wrong," I managed to croak, still gasping for breath. "He never thought of it at all."

"Well, it worked, didn't it!" she shot back at me.

Now I'm very much farther away from my goal, The Piggy whirred. *My hunger to be inside the infected crab is intense. It was very easy for me to use my hyperspace card to put the member of Jrlb's species on the desert planet.*

And I realized then that The Piggy could not only put the parasite back in my brain; it could also put *me* back on J'koot, with all those hungry crabs.

I jumped to my feet and held out The Piggy. "Julian, I've got The Piggy. We've got to get rid of it fast. Throw it away so it will never have contact with another species again!"

"What?" The dinosaur must have felt Julian's shock; it lifted its head, startled. "Have you gone doolally? The Piggy's the prize. If you don't want it, hand it over to me. Throw it away indeed!"

"You don't understand. Please," I begged him. "It's not a prize. It doesn't give anything to anybody. It lies and cheats and brings hell wherever it goes—just to get the sensations it wants."

The dinosaur squirmed in the muck. "What could you *possibly* be talking about?" Julian said. "Whoever doesn't have it at the end of the game will be blasted out of existence."

"A lie. I've played the real game twice and I know. The game doesn't end. No player has ever known the game to end. This is everybody's first game—for hundreds of years. The Piggy just wants to experience one species after another. And it doesn't save *anybody!* Have you ever known the game to end? Have you ever known The Piggy to do anything but create hatred and fighting and cheating and disease and death? Have you?"

Julian didn't say anything.

"And it will kill *me* in a few seconds if we don't get rid of it right away!" I added.

I am very bored now. I do not enjoy being bored.

"Julian!" I said. "Your garbage disposal! The machine that throws away the garbage and makes it invisible and keeps it away from any inhabited planets and anyplace where there's any life at all. Tell the robots to put The Piggy in *there!*"

"You don't think I'd actually *do* that, now do you?" Julian said. "You silly boy. Just give it to me, there's a good chap."

"Barney's right," Katie shouted at him. "Do you really want to go on fighting and killing and chasing and being chased forever? You're not like the others. You're decent. Anyway, you have to do what Barney says or I'll shoot your dinosaur with my crossbow." She took aim.

"You know, now that you put it that way, you might have a point there," Julian said slowly. "I could take naps in here all the time. I wouldn't have to go around being a projection so much. I could just go back to my host's own planet, Voeves, where he'd *really* be comfortable—and better fed, too. Oh, the food there! *So* much more delicious than what's on this ship. I never even thought about it before, but, blimey, it makes a lot of sense."

I look forward to relishing the enjoyment of the crab and its food. Now, The Piggy uttered.

Julian announced an order in another language. A robot pulled a metallic bag out of a dispenser in the wall and ran over to me. I dropped The Piggy into the bag. The robot sealed the bag and rushed it to the round hatchway.

"Desist that command this instant!" Soma ordered.

Where had *she* come from? We spun around.

My heart sank. We were still connected to her ship.

She had simply beamed herself up and walked over here. Her ovipositor was pointed directly at the dinosaur. "My time is now," she continued. "If you do not arrest that command, my babies will be devouring you—for months."

"What makes you think you can talk to me like that?" Julian said. "You overblown insect!"

Julian's robot closed the round hatchway on the silver bag with The Piggy in it. It reached for the button.

"Arrest that command!" Soma shouted, sounding terrified.

"And let you get The Piggy? Think again! I'd rather *nobody* had it!" Julian said.

The robot pushed the button.

The garbage disposal shot The Piggy into the interstellar void at FTL speed. Now it would remain light-years apart from any species forever. That was what it was most afraid of.

I could actually *feel* its presence vanishing. The sensation was like the calming drug at the Death Palace. I realized now that I hadn't really felt relaxed since the aliens had left last summer. Because I had known The Piggy was still active. Now I could hope it was out of the picture for good.

At the same instant the robot pushed the button, Soma's ovipositor arrow pierced the dinosaur's abdomen.

The dinosaur roared with surprise, but it didn't sound like it was in pain. It easily pulled out the arrow with one of its tiny fore claws and dropped it to the floor of its cage. The arrow had not even left any blood. Had it had time to deposit Soma's offspring?

There was a breathless pause. The dinosaur belched and then crouched down. It seemed to have forgotten the arrow already.

And then Julian's projection appeared, in human form. "You bloody bitch!" Julian said irritably to Soma, his hands on his hips. He turned toward Katie and me. "You know how her darling babies work, don't you? They start out by feeding on the more unnecessary parts of the body, so the host will stay alive as long as possible. Do I need to tell you what the *most* unnecessary part of this creature's body is? Me, of course. I'm their target, their first meal. They're drilling their way toward me right this minute. I've got to get out of here! I've got to find a new host immediately."

And then he looked directly at me. "Do you understand, Barney?" Julian said, very slowly and significantly.

"Huh? *Me?*" I said as the ghastly thought sank in. Was he actually asking to live inside *my* intestine, as a way of escaping Soma's babies, who were now infesting the dinosaur?

"Serves you both right!" Soma crowed. "And now I'm going after The Piggy. I will attend it with my porcine locator."

She hurried back to her ship. The connector closed itself. We felt a jolt as her ship lurched away from us.

"She'll never find it, even with her precious porcine locator," Julian said. "She doesn't know how effective my garbage disposal is."

"Can you take us *home* now?" I asked Julian. "Now there's no Piggy to be chased anymore."

"You should really be proud of yourself, Barney,"

Katie said, her face shining. "You helped all sorts of different species by getting rid of that thing."

"Barney, Barney, I need your help. Her loathsome babies have almost reached me!" Julian begged me.

"But . . ." I said, not even wanting to *imagine* it, let alone have it really happen.

Julian was weeping now. "It won't hurt, Barney, I promise. You'll hardly notice. Please, please!" And then he thought of something else. "All it will mean is that you'll be able to eat twice as much—and at the same time you will *lose* all that weight you've gained. And as soon as I get you home I'll find a new host. I promise. You can trust me. Think of how much I helped the two of you."

I turned to Katie. "What am I going to do?" I appealed to her.

Very pale, Katie slumped weakly against the wall. She really hadn't been eating enough, and the last few hours, starting with the escape attempt in disguise, had been very intense. Still, she looked me straight in the eye, resolute. "Well, you *do* need to lose weight, Barney."

"Spot on, lass!" Julian cried.

"But . . ." I objected.

"And he *did* help us."

"And if you *don't*," Julian pointed out, "I'll be sick and dead in a matter of minutes. And then how will you ever get home?"

"That's right, Barney," Katie said, sounding really frightened now.

I groaned. Their arguments were overwhelming. "Okay, okay. What . . . what do I do?"

This part I can't talk about. Katie didn't look. But Julian was right when he said it didn't hurt much. For the first few days, until I got used to it, I mainly just felt an unusual sensation of fullness in my belly. I would lose weight all right.

Julian beamed the cage and the dinosaur separately down to J'koot. His former host would be more comfortable on the surface, and free of its cage—though dying in agony couldn't really be called comfortable. "Poor bloke," Julian said sadly. He was depressed about it for a long time.

But not too depressed to start the ship back toward Earth.

26

Julian's ship was a lot more spacious now, without the huge dinosaur and its cage and its vat of food. It didn't stink nearly as much, either. With Katie around, the trip home was a lot more comfortable and fun than the trip to J'koot had been—even with Julian living inside me. Not to mention we had a whole lot less to worry about.

That didn't mean we weren't worried at all. We'd been away for a long time; no one was really sure how long the days were on J'koot. Adding to that the week and a half trip each way, we could have been gone for several months.

So what were we going to tell our parents? The truth was not a possibility. Of course they wouldn't believe it, and they'd just send me back to that clinic again. Once had been enough. And Katie wasn't eager to go there either.

So how could we explain where we had been for so long? We pondered and discussed it for days.

I also ate a lot of the airplane-type food on Julian's ship, and as he had promised, I steadily lost weight.

It was very difficult to come up with an explanation for our parents. It didn't help that it had been November when we left, so we couldn't say we had just been off hiking—it was way too cold for that.

"Maybe we could tell them we went to Florida," Katie suggested. "And we just kind of camped and hiked around for two months."

"How did we get there?" I asked her.

"We can't say we hitchhiked—then they'd be even *more* furious than they're going to be already. We saved up money and took the bus—that's the cheapest way."

"And maybe we could find a dog somewhere," I said eagerly. "A really big dog, so you'd be nice and comfortable, Julian. Could your robots learn to take care of it?"

"They can be programmed to do almost anything. Yes, a nice big dog might be a hoot. Though it *is* rather nice being able to talk with my host . . ."

"Forget it!" I said instantly. "We're finding a dog ASAP."

When we finally got back into orbit around the Earth, we beamed up one of the biggest dogs we could find, a Great Pyrenees. She was a huge white fluffy animal, about the size of a couch, very cute, and Julian took an instant liking to her.

My weight was back to normal now. It was a wonderful moment when Julian moved into the dog. We named her Julianna, of course.

It turned out we had been gone for just about two

months—that was not long enough for our parents and the police to have given up the search. After we petted Julianna and hugged her and ruffled her luxuriant fur, the robots beamed us back to Katie's apartment, into the backyard of the building, in the middle of the night. From what she said, her parents sounded less uptight than mine.

Of course they were furious, and of course they called my parents instantly. And then we were grounded and in horrible trouble for the rest of that year. But they didn't think we were crazy, the way they thought I was crazy last time. And we didn't have to go back to work—we needed to spend the time instead catching up on our studies. And both sets of parents wanted us at home as much as possible.

They also thought each of us was a bad influence on the other. For a long time Katie and I saw very little of each other.

But after a year or so, that passed, too. From that point on, we were together as much as possible.

Julian had gone back to Voeves after dropping us off. The dog was fine for the time being, but he really preferred a dinosaur—and the cuisine on that planet.

I never forgot what it had felt like to have that parasite inside my brain. And for the first months at home I often wondered what she was doing to Abamee.

But most of all, it was such a relief to know that The Piggy was gone for good. . . .

Epilogue

Madame Gondii was about to give up hope.

She had never felt so demoralized. She didn't understand what was happening. Nothing in her training had prepared her for the strange creature Barney had transformed himself into—and especially not for the round, pink, mechanical entity that he seemed to consider was so terribly important.

Most terrifying and disastrous of all was the behavior of the crabs. They seemed to have lost interest in eating him! And they had been so close, so close! Right next to the fire, about to manacle him to the grill.

And then Barney had started telling them he *wanted* to be eaten. She had done everything she could to make him stop, to make him pretend to be as afraid as an uninfected human would be. But he had somehow learned to ignore her hormones. *Nobody* was supposed to be able to ignore her hormones. How could this human stripling do it?

It was her tragic fate to have been somehow placed in a human being. If she could do her life over again, she would avoid that species at all cost.

But she could not do her life over again.

Yes, she had had a little time to begin to modify her own life cycle. She had retained her ability to reproduce longer than she normally would have. But now she had almost reached the absolute limit. A crab had to eat Barney immediately. But they wouldn't!

Madame Gondii was not the kind of creature who could pretend, or who could lie to herself. She had to face the terrible deadly truth.

She had lost.

She watched helplessly as Barney changed back into a human. She felt a brief moment of hope when he ran back into the grilling chamber. But the crabs seemed to be ill. They just lay there and did nothing to try to eat him. He gathered up the lichen, and then he and his hideous friend began to run. Away from the grilling chamber, away from the crabs, away from any hope for Madame Gondii.

She could feel her body beginning to change. Not laying her eggs was literally a physical pain. Only minutes and she would be incapable of having babies at all. She had never imagined such a disaster could happen to her, after all her hard work. She might as well die.

And then a miracle happened.

She was inside the brain of a crab.

A crab must have eaten Barney's brain after all! She had hardly felt it, it had been very, very quick, but there it was. She was inside a crab.

Home at last!

Convenient as Barney's brain had been, everything in here was so much softer and more comfortable. She also preferred the slimy greenish decor. She snuggled in, relishing every heavenly sensation. Now *this* was real comfort! This was where she belonged.

If she had known how to pray, she would have prayed her thanks.

Triumph and jubilation filled her. She had thought she had lost, but now she had won! She would have her babies after all!

For a moment she allowed herself to bask in the sweet anticipation of motherhood. It was the most wonderful feeling she had ever known.

Then she got down to work. Her tentacles finally began to loosen and stretch. She was full of power now. In minutes, the tentacles had grown and expanded to fill all the interstices of the crab's body. She could finally lay her eggs now, alleviating the deep pain, knowing they would be safe and protected here. And then she could set about altering the crab's reproductive organs so that they could no longer produce crabs, only Madame Gondiis. The gender of the crab was irrelevant to her hormones.

One of her greatest joys was the knowledge that her children would have far, far easier lives than hers. She was an immigrant to the new country, who had suffered and made the perilous voyage herself. And now her chil-

dren would be born in the new country, with all the ben-
efits and none of the ordeals she had gone through.

Because when her babies hatched from the body of
this crab, they would go directly into the bodies of other
crabs. They would not have to endure what she had endured inside a human being. And her children would in
turn reproduce, and have babies that would infect yet
more crabs. On and on down the years it would go.

Madame Gondii did not care about the crabs' culture,
their history, their art and architecture—and the effect
that her children, grandchildren, and her great-great-,
and multi-great-grandchildren would have on the civi-
lization of this world. She only cared about producing
her babies, and fulfilling her function in life.

And how easy it was to control the crab's brain—he
was her slave. Nothing like that recalcitrant human.
How wonderful that Barney was dead and she was finally
rid of him forever!

She wriggled a tentacle and effortlessly released hormones to issue her first command.

Abamee staggered to his feet. The other crabs
watched in horror as he lurched blindly out of the
grilling chamber. Madame Toxoplasma Gondii directed
him to the kitchen. He pushed the chefs out of the way
and began shoving food into his mouth, not even using
utensils, concentrating on protein and carbohydrates,
for the babies. The chefs backed fearfully out of the
room.

After Madame Toxoplasma Gondii filled him up, she
sent him to bed—and he began to have her babies. She
had already altered his reproductive organs, and out

floated her first airborne offspring, no bigger than the head of a pin. And then came another, and another. Madame Toxoplasma Gondii's children were here at last.

Soon there were dozens, hundreds of them. They floated on little balloons made of threadlike fibers.

The first one wafted over to Abamee's head. "Hello," it said, in a voice so small Abamee could barely hear it. It waved one of its many legs at Abamee. "Our mother is your friend."

Abamee knew its mother was not really his friend. He also knew—he could feel it through his entire body— that he must do nothing to go against her plans, or he would suffer the consequences. "What . . . what are you going to do?" he asked her baby.

"We are going to make homes for ourselves," it said in its sweet voice.

"But where?" Abamee asked, even though he knew the terrible answer already.

"Where the breeze takes us. Up, down. South, north. But always, always, to another one of our friends like you."

The babies could not stay unprotected for long. They drifted, so small as to be almost invisible, to other crabs. They landed on the crabs' heads and excreted acid to form lesions there, into which they crawled, and began making their homes inside.

And now Madame Toxoplasma Gondii could truly relax for the first time in her life, knowing her babies were finally safe. She had achieved her goal.

As for what it felt like for Abamee to be infected by

her—and what it would feel like for all the other crabs who were now being infected—that was not something that interested her.

But it *was* something that interested The Piggy. Too bad The Piggy would never be able to experience it.

Or would it?